John Whitbourn ha[...]
published in the U[...]
after winning the BB[...]
First Fantasy No[...]
Dangerous Energy in 1991.

Most recently, his published works
include the *Downs-Lord* trilogy
concerning the establishment of empire
in an alternative, monster-ridden
England. Whitbourn's works have
received favourable reviews in *The Times*,
Telegraph, and *Guardian*, amongst others.

A former archaeologist and British civil
servant, he lives in at least one of the
several parallel Binscombes.

Also by John Whitbourn

A Dangerous Energy
Popes & Phantoms
To Build Jerusalem
The Royal Changeling
Downs-Lord Dawn
Downs-Lord Day
Downs-Lord Doomsday
Frankenstein's Legions

Binscombe Tales

VOLUME ONE

John Whitbourn

Spark Furnace Books

Published 2011 by Spark Furnace Books,
an imprint of Fabled Lands LLP
www.sparkfurnace.com

ISBN 978-0-9567372-6-7

CONTENTS

Introduction

All that a reader need know about me is that I'm struggling up the shore of middle age, living with my wife, Liz, my son, Joseph and daughters, Rebecca and Esther, in a part of the South country where the graveyards and old records are littered, over the last four centuries or so, with strangers bearing my surname. Beyond that there is silence, but I suspect we go back still further.

Apart from the above, I will largely leave it to others to speak for me and the Binscombe Tales. These are stories about the 'least vivacious'[1] and 'most threatened'[2] people in the world—the aboriginal South-east English. They concern a mythical village where strangers are welcome—but not always safe. The cast comprises: 'men of modest means and ancient principles'[3]. Possible alternative titles were *Greenbelt Gothic* and *Tales from Tomorrow-land*[4]. To sum, the spirit which imbues them is best expressed thus:

> On the surface, there was always an impeccably realistic world, but underneath, behind the backdrop's cracked canvas, lurked something different, something mysterious or abstract. On the surface, an

[1] Matthew Engel, *The Guardian* May 1988

[2] Sonia Morozov, political commentator (1958–)

[3] Oliver Cromwell (1599–1658)

[4] 1980s Government parlance for the South East

intelligible lie, underneath, the unintelligible truth.[5]

And

> Our history in these islands is too tragical to think about. We have abandoned its reality, and taken to a myth which is useful for stabilising the State.[6]

It just strikes me that the English are losing sight of their history, that is to say, the vital perceived links between past, present and future—and, just as importantly, their shared mythology. I also gibe at the growing Americanisation and 'Londonisation' of everything. The Binscombe Tales emanate from that vague *sense* of *loss*. They perhaps seek to prompt an alternative perception of life in *England* (and Britain, I suppose). They also arise, so I've been assured, from 'the twin streams of human consciousness; thoughts of here and—somewhere else'.[7]

As to the stories' setting, I can wax more loquacious: 'About Zion I will not be silent, About Jerusalem I will not grow weary.'[8]

There is, more or less, a real place called Binscombe, born perhaps in the Iron age, if not earlier, adopted by the Romans (and ending badly), then refounded by our own Abraham, Buden the Saxon. Though definitely around by then, the Domesday Book, the Norman's loot-tally, looked straight

---

[5] Milan Kundera (1929–), *The Unbearable Lightness of Being,* 1984

[6] Peter Levi (1931–2000), *The Flutes of Autumn,* 1983

[7] Professor E Griffiths, classicist, philosopher, Celtic Marxist and *bon viveur* (?–)

[8] Isaiah 62:1

through us—and there, doubtless hangs a tale. It was thus not until 1227 that Binscombe felt ready to stride, gorgeous and pouting, onto the world stage (well, the *Rotuli Litterarum Clausarum*) for its first written reference.

Amidst all the only-to-be-expected mundanity, it has interesting features—like most places if you only look. Nearby are—in the 'old tongue'—Dragon Hill and Wild Cat Hill and Witch's Valley. The pagan gods lingered longer here, and left a renowned group of missionary-proof place names like Tue(*Tiw*)eley, Thur(*Thor?*)sley. A suspicious looking bump bides unregarded in the landscape, perhaps a second Silbury Hill awaiting its Howard Carter.

And on that landscape trod people; remarkable people, such as Theophilus Oglelthorpe, valiant soldier and Jacobite, duellist and all-round English-icon who had the good taste to buy Binscombe Manor. In 1685 his mad cavalry charge into Keynsham changed the course of English history, and the great truism 'dead men tell no tales' may be attributable to him.

Back when the Quakers were dangerous radicals, their founder, George Fox, came to Binscombe and the barn he preached in still bears his name. As a result we even have our very own martyr, done in by the Church of England back in 1660. Thomas Patching of Binscombe Farm heard Fox's words and took them to heart, dying in a foreign land (Kingston-upon-Thames gaol) accordingly. His body, brought home, now rests (one trusts) in the old Quaker burial ground beside that very barn.

Not far away, a woman astounded the eighteenth century by giving birth to rabbits (we have her word on it). Here the telegraphist-hero, Jack Phillips, of RMS *Titanic* fame, grew up and became what he was.

A short way down the road, in a hamlet still isolated and obscure, a lone Saxon retained his land even after the Norman ethnic cleansing. And a 'person' of sorts (no less revered), the Surrey Puma— indigenous, mysterious and never-yet caught—prowls round about.

There is a working men's club, known as the Moscow, and old men with Anglo-Saxon names like Æethelbert. Many family trees verge onto that interesting time before records, and the same old names roll on through the centuries. They are still here. Faint hope arises that the real Doomsday will find them so.

'They all come back', the local saying maintains and, property prices and gentrification notwithstanding, it remains broadly true. I did.

These two Binscombes, literary and amalgam-actual, are not the same, but they are linked with subtle and invisible bridges of 'what if?'. Similarly, I have yet to meet Mr Disvan here but his spirit seems ever present—so I don't rule out the possibility.

However, the truth of the matter is that:

(i) these are just 'ghost stories' which I hope you enjoy.

and

(ii) *God gives all men, all earth to love*
But since man's heart is small,
Ordains for each one spot shall prove,
Beloved over all. [9]

John Whitbourn
Binscombe
December 1997

---

[9] Rudyard Kipling (1865–1936)

Another Place

Tired of unpacking and arranging furniture, I decided to take a brief preliminary look around my new village. Traipsing at random along the quiet streets I came, at length, to the recreation ground and seeing a cricket match in progress decided to watch for a short while. It was also perhaps in my mind that I might pass a social word or two concerning the weather or progress of play with my fellow villagers. For the foreseeable future this place was to be my home and it was desirable that I should get to know some people so as to start the long process of becoming accepted.

The 'Rec' (as I was told the locals termed it) had very distinct physical boundaries. On one side its expanse was stopped dead by the edge of a lake and opposite what passed for a major road in these parts, together with a fence and a screen of tall fir trees, separated the grass from the outer frontier of the housing estates. The rest of the Rec's containing box comprised, on one side, the new and brutal high wall of a secondary modern school and on the other, an ancient and even higher wall protecting some of the village's original houses from curiosity and cricket balls.

In between the trees on the road-side were interspersed some wooden benches on which spectators were sitting and it was to these that I crossed over. Not all of the seats were occupied and should I have so wished I could have sat alone. However, for the reasons given above, I chose to join an elderly man on a bench which gave a clear view of the pavilion, pitch and scoreboard. Beside the seat were sprawled a number of young lads, their BMX and Chopper bikes beside them, who were playing only occasional attention to the game in progress.

No one looked up at my arrival or paid any heed to me at all and, though I put on my most amiable and approachable expression in the hope that a conversation might ensue, the local silence was maintained. Eventually my attention was caught up in the cricket (passably good for village standard I thought) and an hour passed quickly and imperceptibly by.

The church clock striking seven broke my reverie and caused me to recall the state of unfettered anarchy my house was in. Tomorrow was a working day and so a great deal of progress remained to be made that very evening: meeting the natives must therefore await another occasion.

Then, just as I got up to go, the old man with whom I'd shared the bench spoke although he did not turn his head or take his eyes from the match.

'Are you a newcomer?' he asked.

I wondered for a second if it was indeed me he was addressing for he'd already had ample opportunity to put the question before. However, seeing that the children were the only other people in immediate earshot, I assumed I must be the one spoken to and replied accordingly.

'Yes, I am.'

He looked round in a most friendly manner.

'Nice to meet you and welcome to Binscombe. I'm Mr Disvan.'

'How do you do, Mr Disvan. My name's Oakley.'

He pondered this for a longer time than the mere revelation of my name strictly justified but appeared to come to no conclusion about it for the time being.

'Do you like cricket, Mr Oakley?'

'In moderation.'

He smiled: 'My feelings entirely. What is your sport, then?'

'Well, I don't really have one as such. I quite like backgammon... and darts.'

'Oh well, they're good enough games—especially darts. You'll not lack for companions around here I'm thinking.'

'No?'

'Some of the people hereabouts only live for darts and everything else is an intrusion. Go into the Duke of Argyll on a Friday night and you'll see what I mean.'

I couldn't think of a sensible sounding answer to this and so silence returned. It stretched out into a full minute or so and I was once more on the point of taking my leave when the old man spoke again: this time with a note of great seriousness in his voice.

'Where exactly is it you've moved to, Mr Oakley?'

'Binscombe Crescent.'

Mr Disvan continued looking straight ahead but the young cyclists, hitherto oblivious to our presence and conversation, stopped their chat and, as one, stared directly at me. Almost involuntarily I returned their stares. They in turn looked to Mr Disvan as if for guidance and then, finding none there, returned instantly to juvenile banter.

I found it hard to accept that this scene had actually occurred. Could they have misheard my reply and imagined it to be something outrageous? In any event, the old man's voice, when he spoke again, had not changed its tone.

'Yes, I'd heard there'd been a change down at Binscombe Crescent. What number is it you've bought, may I ask?'

I told him the house.

'I know it well; built middle fifties. Mr and Mrs Trevisan lived there and then, in his turn, their son Daniel. He works up North now.'

'Slough, actually.'

'Yes, that's right. Slough or some such place. Presumably, it was Daniel that sold it to you.'

'Yes.'

'Very nice house.'

'Thank you.'

'Well, Mr Oakley, I mustn't keep you any longer. It's been a pleasure meeting you and I hope you'll settle in happily very soon. No doubt we shall bump into each other again before long,'

'Yes, no doubt.'

And so saying I went back to my wearisome work.

* * *

Months elapsed before I saw Mr Disvan again; a fact that I thought distinctly odd considering the size of the village. Several times I enquired after him and publican and shopkeeper alike would say something along the lines of: 'Oh yes, he's about all right, I saw him only yesterday. Perhaps you'll see him tomorrow.'

Curiously enough, however, his paths never seemed to cross my line of vision even though all my evenings and weekends were spent in Binscombe. Accordingly, he had almost faded from my memory when, entering the Duke of Argyll one night, I was surprised to see him sitting peaceably in the corner by the chimney stack and the charity-bound tower of ten-pence pieces. On the small round table before him was a vast bound book and a glass of something dark. My path to the bar took me past that particular corner and so I greeted him as I went by.

'Evening, Mr Disvan; how are you? Haven't seen you for a long while.'

'Nor I you. Pleased to meet you again.'

Being English, neither of us presumed to transform our cordial greeting into conversation on the basis of so casual an acquaintance. Therefore I carried on up to the bar and spoke similar hellos to the familiar faces there.

In the interval since my arrival I'd managed to make several friends by means of assiduous and persistent socialising but it so happened that none of them were present that night and so I drank alone.

It should not be thought that the people of Binscombe were unapproachable or hostile to strangers, for they were not. Nearly every person I'd come into contact with in the course of my short stay had been friendly or, at worse, benevolently neutral in their attitude towards me. But even so, although there must have been two dozen villagers with whom I was on 'good morning terms', even with these there seemed a point of familiarity beyond which only the elapse of time could grant me pass. I attached little importance to it. Their insularity was not an intended rebuff to me but merely something natural, even in so urbanised a place as Binscombe.

Thus, I sat at the bar with half a dozen other men in contemplative quiet whilst consuming a few pints and considering the decorative tasks still to done in my house. It was this silence that caused my eye to wander about the interior of the Argyll seeking diversion and noting, for the first time really, its plain and traditional furnishings. There wasn't much to catch or grab a gaze: pictures of long deceased local football teams, obscure trophies and prints of the last king but two—that sort of thing. All else was functional and solely intended to facilitate social drinking and therefore it took little time for my attention to return, uninspired, to its starting point.

It was then that I noticed the full but apparently ownerless glass on the bar beside me. There was nothing unusual about this in itself, for customers often popped out to make a phone call or see a friend in the saloon. However, when a full fifteen minutes elapsed without anyone returning to claim the drink, I felt moved, for conversation's sake if nothing else, to mention it to the landlord.

'Didn't someone like your beer?' I asked, nodding towards the lonely pint of bitter.

Strangely for a normally talkative and cheerful sort of host, the landlord wasn't drawn by my question. He didn't look up from his glass washing and said, in a manner that was almost curt:

'Maybe not.'

No one around the bar, though in easy hearing distance, betrayed so much as a sign of having heard my quip; no one even looked towards me or the glass in question. If commonsense hadn't dictated otherwise, I could well have believed that I'd said something wrong.

It was this half felt sense of solecism that caused me to think that I should retreat from the bar and join Mr Disvan for a few words before adjourning home. An unmistakable air of unease had entered my social evening but since I felt that its creation was none of my doing I didn't consider it proper to leave straightaway.

Fortunately, Mr Disvan seemed disposed to entertain company and pulled up a chair for me when he saw me approaching.

'Can I ask what it is you're reading?' I said.

By way of reply he lifted the large hardback book up and presented it spine-wards towards me so that

I could read the title: *THE HOLY KORAN*.

This was a hard thing to make an adequate response to.

'I see... I've never read it myself.'

'No?' he replied.

'No' I answered weakly, whilst hoping that a topic of conversation would suddenly and miraculously occur to me. In the event, the old man came to my rescue and provided one.

'And what do you think of our area now you're settled in, Mr Oakley?'

'I like it very much.'

'Good.'

'And in a sense it was a home area to me already.'

'In what way?'

'My family lived in this village for centuries, so I've been told; before moving away in my grandfather's time.'

'That's right. I thought your name was familiar when I spoke to you at the cricket match. There's been Oakleys here since records were kept and for goodness knows how long in the time before—the time before records I mean,' he added hastily.

'Are you a local historian, Mr Disvan?'

'Of a sort, Mr Oakley; in some specific fields. For instance, I know of your great-grandfather on the paternal side, Malachai Oakley, a carpenter. Then before him was his father, Jacob Evelyn Oakley, publican and churchwarden (an unusual mix in those days). If you were to press me I could probably recite you a dozen successive generations of Oakleys, all by name and occupation.' He looked keenly at me over the edge of his raised glass. 'And now you're back.'

I was still winding in this hitherto unknown genealogical information but felt obliged to agree with his last words even though, at that point, I'd no intention of remaining for another twelve generations.

'Yes, I suppose I am.' I said. 'Look, what you say is fascinating, Mr Disvan but how on earth did you acquire such detailed knowledge?'

'Its not so difficult. Everyone knows everything about everybody here and in Binscombe memories are powerful strong.'

The evidence of my local ties and Disvan's close familiarity with them emboldened me enough to ask him the question which had inexplicably frozen the atmosphere at the bar:

'Tell me, Mr Disvan,' (this in a lowered voice), 'why has that pint of beer been left standing on the bar? Why doesn't the landlord clear it away if it's been abandoned?'

'It's not abandoned. It's Mr Bolding's drink. It won't be tipped away until closing time.'

'Won't Mr Bolding drink it?'

Disvan smiled warmly, 'I very much doubt it. Not where he is.'

'I don't understand. Where is Mr Bolding then?'

'He's in the other Binscombe.'

'I beg your pardon?'

'The other Binscombe.'

'Where's that?'

The old man smiled again. 'That's a very good question. All I can say with any degree of sureness is that, on the anniversary of Mr Bolding going there, we place a commemorative drink where he always used to stand at the bar.'

'Commemorative? Is he dead?'

'Oh, I shouldn't think so. It was only ten years ago he went and he was in his middle forties then.'

I must have appeared a picture of puzzlement. 'I'm sorry but I still don't understand,' I said.

Mr Disvan disregarded that and changed the tack

of the conversation without warning. 'Did your grandfather ever say much to you about Binscombe, Mr Oakley?'

'He died when I was very small.'

'Ah. I see.'

'But you haven't explained about Mr Bolding.'

'No, I haven't.'

'Well, aren't you going to?'

'If you wish.'

'Yes please.'

Disvan looked at the bar and then at me.

'The explanation isn't very instructive or edifying.'

'Even so.'

'Very well then, I will tell you. Only not now, for I have to go, and it's a long story.'

'Is there something wrong about it?' I said hurriedly, for Disvan was drinking up and preparing to put his coat on.

'Wrong? No, not wrong as such but, as I've said, it's a long story. The next time we meet up I'll recount it to you.'

'Okay.'

And with that, Disvan tucked the Koran under his arm and left.

I stayed a little longer to ponder the lessons of the day and the portents for the morrow whilst enjoying another drink. Nevertheless, no matter how hard I thought of work and love and plans I found my gaze turning, time and time again, to the solitary glass and the empty space at the bar.

* * *

After that evening I looked out for Mr Disvan with some considerable animation, for I keenly wished to hear the story with which I'd been tantalised. Therefore, after a week of his non-appearance at the Argyll (or anywhere else for that matter) I turned again to questioning tradesmen and other local 'in the know' people as to his whereabouts. However, just as before, I was told that he was 'around' as normal and had been seen, spoken to even, only yesterday. But to-day? No, they didn't know.

It was a very annoying process but my curiosity was such that I only desisted from enquiries when I realised that I was making myself appear an obsessive in front of the people with whom I had to live. Paradoxically enough, therefore, the day after I resolved to put the matter out of my mind, I managed to run the elusive Mr Disvan to ground again. I was going about my customary evening stroll which would presumably end in the Argyll, when I thought I recognised the old man's distinctive Panama hat atop a figure sitting in the recreation ground.

Without needing to consider the matter, I hurried over to the spot and saw that it was indeed the person I'd been looking for. He was resting on a bench that stood in a corner which, lacking proper nets, the local cricket team employed as a practise area. He appeared to be watching the half dozen men who were currently using it for this purpose. I came up and sat beside him and although he did not turn around he seemed to know who had arrived.

'Hello again, Mr Oakley.'

'Hello.'

'You have the air of being on a mission.'

'Do I?'

'Indeed. Very much a man with a purpose.'

'Well, now you come to mention it, I was rather hoping you'd very belatedly finish telling the story about Mr Bolding's drink.'

'Oh, that old tale. That's your local roots coming

through you know—curiosity about such trifles!' His tone was jocular rather than admonitory.

'I can't answer as to that but I'd certainly like to have the mystery cleared up.'

Disvan turned to observe me, his face and voice suddenly very serious. 'Oh no, that I can't do. I doubt anybody could. But I can tell you the story if you really want.'

He looked round at two young men who'd come and sat down on the grass not far off in order to adjust pads and rebind a bat handle.

'This is not for your ears,' he said to them, and to my surprise they instantly got up and moved out of earshot without so much as a word of protest. Thereafter we were left to ourselves.

'Is it that bad?' I asked.

'No, not bad or wrong as I said to you before but,' he added wistfully, 'it's something you should be selective about who you tell.'

These pseudo-warnings, such as preceded horror films or shocking newsreels on the television, only ever served to whet my appetite for what was to come and I was accordingly now all agog.

'Where did Mr Bolding live before he went away?' I asked.

'Binscombe Crescent.'

'Just as I suspected. What number?'

'That needn't concern you; rest assured it wasn't where you now live.'

'If he had lived in my house why should that concern me?'

'Because of the thought you might follow him.'

'To the other Binscombe?'

'Perhaps, or even to somewhere else.'

'So what is the full story, Mr Disvan?'

'Like I've said, I don't think anyone, with the

possible exception of Bolding himself, knows what you call the full story. I only know the beginning.'

'Which is?'

'Which is that one day Bolding vanished for a full forty-eight hours. Now, he was a locksmith and clock repairer by trade and he had a little shop in the main street. It's a toy shop now; doubtless you'll have seen it. Anyway, what with the shop not opening and people wanting keys cut and the like, it was soon noticed that he wasn't about. Mrs Bolding—she was seen out shopping and so on but she never mentioned anything so folks didn't enquire.

It was all very strange though, because every night of his life, from the day he left school at fourteen, he always popped into the Argyll of an evening. The licensing laws were easier in those days and the policeman was a local boy. Suddenly, two nights running, he didn't show up and people began to think he'd run away or Mrs Bolding had done him in (for there was no love lost between the two) or something like that.'

'And...'

'And it got to the point where we considered getting Stan the constable to look into it even though we were reluctant to interfere. Then, sure enough, Bolding turned up at the Argyll the very next evening and the mystery was solved. Or so we thought then.'

'How do you mean?'

Well, he was pale and sickly looking and unshaven. It seemed obvious he'd been unwell.'

'And hadn't he been?'

'No, he'd been as fit as a fiddle, so he told us. The point was, you see, that Mr Bolding was one of the old sort—a very upright, truthful sort of man. He was an elder of the Methodist lot and whatever you may think of them it still does count for something. If anyone asked him a question he'd always give the straight honest truth without deception. That was the way he was; he didn't think he had any choice in the matter you understand. It was how he'd built up a nice little business. People took their custom to him because they knew they could trust him.'

'What did he say, then?'

'Well, old man Yarum went up to him and says, "Ho Jack, where've you been? Sick? You look like death warmed up!" And blow me if he didn't. "No," he says, "I've not been ill, I've been away." "Away where?" we asked, and he answered, "I'm not sure."

'As you might imagine, we didn't quite know what to make of that for he wasn't what you would call a heavy drinking man. Accordingly we asked what he was on about but he wouldn't give an explanation. He had his usual couple of drinks without another word and then went home—still looking like a ghost.'

'Did he ever say where he'd been?'

'At that point he wasn't able to, for he wasn't sure himself. As I've said, Jack Bolding was a painfully honest man, if nothing else, and if he said that he didn't know where he'd been then he really didn't.'

'But he found out later, did he?'

'Well, let's just say he had his suspicions confirmed and his remaining hopes torn away—and by that time he was a very troubled as well as a very honest man.'

'Why?'

'Because that was only the first time he disappeared. It happened again only a month and a bit later and then once again a couple of weeks after that. His shop was closed up for days on each occasion and his absence was very noticeable, he being such a regular chap in his habits. Each time he'd come back looking worse than ever and he'd refuse to talk about it to anyone. In fact he got quite short with people who enquired after him even though he was normally a civil type.'

'What happened then?'

'Well, things were plainly going badly with him. His skin was pallid and he'd lost so much weight that his clothes hung on him like sheets. Mrs Bolding wasn't the sort of person he could take his problems to so the lads said to me: "Mr Disvan, you have a word with poor old Jack." So I did.'

'What did he say?'

'Not much at first. I went up to him at a cricket match—versus Brightstone as I recall—and I said, "Come on Jack, out with it. What's haunting you these days?" Well, he turned round and replied, "Why don't you all mind your own b---- business?" Which wasn't like him at all. Anyway, he must have thought about it and realised that sort of language wasn't called for and how we all meant well, for he came back to me soon after and apologised. Not that I minded of course, for I'd known Bolding a long time and I could see from his weary eyes that he was bearing a mighty burden.'

'So did he confide in you?'

'Not on that occasion but a week after, when he'd vanished once more and then reappeared three days later, I approached him again and found that he was now keen to talk. "Disvan," he said, "I've got to speak to someone or I think I'm going to lose my wits." "Talk away as much as you like," I said and took him to my house for a cup of tea.'

'Did he manage to explain what was happening?'

'He tried. "I've been away," he says. "I don't know why, I don't know how and I don't know where to." This naturally puzzled me, although I had to accept his statement, and when I asked him what he meant he gave the same answer—"for I can't give any better," were his words. I kept on probing, though, for I felt sorry for him and bit by bit he told the story.'

'Which was?'

'Which was that one day, just like any other day, he shut up his shop and went home for his midday meal. He ate it, said goodbye to his wife and went out of his front door—into another place.'

'Did he explain that?'

'Oh yes, in great detail.'

'What sort of other place was it he'd walked into then?'

'He said he was still in Binscombe, yet at the same time he wasn't because it was no Binscombe he'd ever seen.'

'I don't understand.'

'Neither did he, poor fellow. Neither does anyone, but there it still is. Like I keep on saying, Bolding was an honest man and if he said that he'd stumbled into another world then you're safe in accepting he did.'

'What was it like?'

'Empty. It was the Binscombe he'd known all his life but deserted and ruined. He mentioned that quite specifically. All the houses and shops had been wrecked or fallen down of their own accord. Apparently the recreation ground in that other Binscombe was chest high in grass and there were bushes and weeds in the roadways.'

'What did he do?'

'Just what you'd expect. He stepped back inside sharpish!'

'And?'

'And for an instant he said he could still hear the sounds of his wife clearing up in the kitchen but then that faded and died and he found himself in a ruined house. It was his house right enough, but the roof was half gone and there was ivy and moss on the inside walls.'

'And he panicked?'

'No. Bolding wasn't like that. Not a man of strong passions at all. Apparently he checked what was left of the place just to see if Mrs Bolding was there but she wasn't. He said that all through the house he saw things that were his, all scattered about and broken, so there couldn't be any doubt left as to whose dwelling he was in.'

'And there was no one around at all?'

'No, no one. He went to the neighbour's houses and knocked on their doors, save one that no longer had a door, and got no answer. Judging by appearances he said that it didn't look as if there'd been anyone living in them for many a year.

'So anyway, off he went to his shop—a natural enough reaction for a small trader—and all along the way there was the same story: ruin and desolation, jungle and neglect. He couldn't believe his eyes, poor man. He thought it must be some horrible dream he was trapped in.'

'But I presume it wasn't.'

'I don't see how it could have been. A man can't disappear into a dream for days on end, can he?'

'I suppose not.'

'No. So there he is, in Binscombe High Street, surveying the clumps of grass sprouting up through the middle of the road, half the buildings tumbled down and not so much as a sign of a human being anywhere. Soon enough he went to look at his shop and found that there was a young sapling growing out of the front window. Well, you can imagine how he felt on seeing that.

'His sign was still there over the front and some stock remained on display but otherwise the place was a shambles. That little shop was his life really and seeing it in such a state affected him more than anything else he'd seen so far, or so he told me. It was then you could be uncharitable enough to say that he panicked, insofar as Jack knew how to.'

'What did he do?'

'He went straight back home, trying to ignore the unearthly hush, found a dry spot and went to sleep for twelve hours solid. A nervous reaction I suppose.'

'And when he woke?'

'He opened his eyes, cautiously hoping it had all been a dream after all but he soon saw that wasn't so. The roof was still full of holes and he could see the stars as he lay there. When he looked out of the front door again there was the village, albeit in darkness, but not a single light visible from horizon to horizon. The whole countryside was as black as pitch.

Anyway, to keep himself occupied he had a scout around the house (the roof let in a lot of moonlight) and in his travels he found a calendar—one of those tear-off, day by day types.'

'Which said?'

'March twenty-third, 1965. So at least five years must have elapsed between anyone paying any attention to it and Bolding's arrival. He said that sort of time gap seemed to tie in with the decay he'd seen all about. Next he looked for a newspaper or such like to see if any further light could be shed on the mystery, but time and wind and rain must have dealt with them all for he never did find one even later on, when he ventured further afield.'

'So he went exploring, did he?'

'What else could he do? Hour after hour passed and he got fed up sifting through the junk in his house, so when the sun came up he went for a walk.'

'Where?'

'All over. He cut a path across the recreation ground to the edge of the Lake—full of fish he said, now that there was no one to catch them. And then he worked his way round the edge to the Old Manor House. By the looks of it someone had shot that up and then burnt it, and seeing that made him feel wary and suspicious. In due course he walked all the way to Goldenford and took a shotgun and ammunition from the storeroom at Jeffrey Brothers. With that by him he felt a bit safer.

'All the same it must have been a disquieting journey. He said that even the main roads were overgrown and that the town bridge was fallen down so he had to chance the old ford to get into the High Street. Standing at the top of the town, he could see the whole place was in just as bad a state as Binscombe—weeds growing up between the setts, shop windows caved in, roofs collapsed. Just total ruin, in fact, and over everything was that great silence.'

'And no people there either?'

'No people, no cats, no dogs. Apart from the birds flying overhead and a few cows on a hill in the distance, there was nothing moving at all.'

'Did he ever find out where everyone had gone?'

'Ah, now you're jumping ahead of the story.'

'Sorry.'

'Anyway, back he walks to Binscombe, jumping at shadows and clutching his gun, but once again he sees not a soul. By now he was really upset and once he was home he barricaded himself in and curled up to sleep in the same corner as before.'

'And..?'

'And that's where his wife found him the next morning. "What the devil are you doing sleeping on the hallway floor in all your clothes?" she said. "And where did you get that gun?"'

'He was back.'

'Precisely. Well, up he gets and dashes outside. When he saw that there were cars and passers-by and that the roads and houses were well kept up and lived in, he could have wept for joy, so he told me. He turned round to look at his own house and saw that the roof was whole and the chimney in an upright position once more and only then, I think, was he fully convinced that he'd returned to the world he knew. Following on from that he realised what a state he was in and what a picture he looked standing gawping in the front garden with a shotgun in his hands. People were beginning to stare so he quickly nipped back inside.'

'What did he tell his wife?'

'Nothing, I don't think. As I've said, whatever love they might once have had was long since dead and buried and they didn't even talk much anymore. Apparently she assumed he'd been off with a fancy woman whilst he was away, not that she cared over-much, and it was easier for him not to correct her. Anyhow, he got her to make him a meal and directly after he came to the Argyll for something to steady his nerves—which was when we all saw him as I described to you before.'

'What happened then?'

'Well, at first he could hardly bring himself to accept what had occurred as reality but there was the small matter of the shotgun which he now had and hadn't owned before. He couldn't discount that as imagination. Understandably, he put the whole business out of his mind and tried to get on with life as best he could. Not being an unduly reflective sort of man helped him with that and he said that he eventually felt safe and normal again when...'

'He went back.'

'That's right. He was alone in his shop in the middle of the morning and bent down to get something out of a box below the counter. When he straightened up again and looked out of the window, everything had changed. The bank and the chemist's shop opposite were all tumble-down, the pedestrians and shoppers had vanished and there was just that almighty quiet left. His shop looked like a whirlwind had been through it and the sapling was back growing out of the floor and through the broken shop front.'

'How did he react?'

'He went straight to the Argyll, broke in and drank a bottle of brandy he found there. After he'd slept that off, he cleaned the bar billiards table up and played game after game into the night—anything to keep his mind off his location I suppose. Eventually he went back to the shop, the next morning presumably, and fell asleep again through sheer nervous exhaustion. When he woke up he found he was back in our Binscombe. Apparently his wife had come along the previous day, found him missing and locked the place up herself.'

'What did he do this time?'

'All sorts of things, since he had to take it seriously now. He went to see his priest or pastor or whatever it is the Methodists call their top people but the man turned out to be of a modernistic frame of mind. He asked whether he had problems with his sex life and referred him to a psychiatrist friend. Naturally Bolding wouldn't hold with that sort of business so he went and tried to get the local C of E man to exorcise him but they don't believe in such things anymore, or so the vicar said. Eventually, in his desperation, he ended up going to see one of the gypsy (well, Diddecoi really) wise-women at Epsom but she refused to take his money.'

'Why?'

'He was being hunted, she said. Another place had claimed him and was drawing closer all the time and there was nothing he could do to change or even delay the matter. She told him to accept gracefully the place that fate had prepared for him and, if he could, to be thankful lest his opposition should bring further misfortune.'

'And did he accept it? Was he thankful?'

'Would you? Would you be? Women like her perhaps know things that we don't, unless they're all just clever fakes as many say, and maybe they see things differently as a result. However that may be, Jack Bolding was stuck as he was and resignation to fate and all that stuff wasn't really his way. So no, he didn't accept or give thanks. In the event, though, he might just as well have done because, whether he accepted it or not, there was precious little he could do about it other than to try and stay in company at all times.'

'But that didn't work?'

'Possibly it did. Leastways he never crossed over when he was with a crowd of people or when someone was looking at him. Even so his travels continued.'

'Just as before?'

'Exactly as before because, try as you might, you can't spend every minute of the day in company. Well, not and live a normal, bearable life at the same time. So, to give you some examples: once he woke up and found himself in the other Binscombe. Another time he came out of the garden privy and discovered he'd crossed over. If he was gardening or taking a stroll he couldn't be sure that his very next step wouldn't be into the other place. By this stage he'd gone over maybe a dozen times for around one to three days apiece. His wife was quite convinced he was seeing another woman.'

'How did he deal with that?'

'He said, "I only wish I were—or a man or boy or donkey!" and she took that funny as you might expect. Mind you, Bolding had been dining on nothing but tongue-pie and cold shoulder from her since she found the shop unattended so it didn't make much of a difference to the situation between them.'

'What did he do during these trips?'

'Explore or drink or weep or despair according to his mood. On one occasion he said that he went as far as London on a bicycle he'd found. Well, that's over thirty miles or more!'

'How was London?'

'The same as everywhere else.'

'Didn't he find anyone?'

'No. He did say that one night he saw a light in the far distance but it only lasted a few seconds and he said it might have been just wishful thinking on his part.'

'What else did he say?'

'That Waterloo Bridge had been dynamited by the looks of what remained, and Big Ben was also down. There was no sign of life whatsoever in the City. It was as if everyone had upped and gone one day and there'd not been a single visitor since, until he arrived. Anyway, as I recall, he said that he went and wandered round the British Museum for a while, for want of anything better to do. Then he dined on some tinned food from the Savoy and ended up sleeping under Nelson's protection in Trafalgar Square. The next thing he knew was being woken up by a policeman and arrested for vagrancy—in our world, needless to say.'

'So how did it all end?'

'Well, strangely enough, it was possible that the gypsy woman was at least partially right. Perhaps the other Binscombe was coming ever closer to Mr Bolding because each occasion he went there he was staying longer and longer. As you can imagine, his health and nerves were suffering, not to mention his business. That was shut up half the time since he was either over in the other place or too worried about going there to devote his mind to work. His trade was drifting away, as you might expect, his wife wasn't talking to him and was fit to leave him at any minute because of the ideas she'd got in her head which he wasn't able to correct, and generally speaking he felt his role, his reason for being in this world if you like, was dwindling away.

'So, in the end, he had to give some attention to the life he was leading, willing or no, in the other Binscombe. After all, he was spending a lot of time over there by this stage. Accordingly, he mended the roof of his house and dug the garden over so he could plant vegetables—otherwise he was likely to starve for there wasn't much food to be found. Apparently he went on foraging expeditions, sometimes as far as Croydon or Winchester, on his bike and he'd be away from the house—the one in the other place that is—for days on end. London he henceforth avoided since he said it gave him the creeps to see that, of all places, overgrown and silent as it was.

'In time he found most of the tools and suchlike that he needed to survive and he also ransacked a few shops to refurnish his house in finer style than it had ever been in our world! He said he even managed to find an old wind-up gramophone to give him a bit of company.'

'It sounds almost cosy.'

'Well I wouldn't say that exactly. His little, inhabited, cultivated spot was set in a great quiet jungle, so to speak, and I don't think his life can have been easy. I mean, how could you feel at home in that situation?

'Anyhow, during the times that he was in our world, he took to filling his pockets with seeds and shotgun cartridges and suchlike useful things so that when he crossed over again he'd have something to add to his stores. The point was, you see, that he was growing less and less sure that he ever was coming back here to stay.'

'Apart from you and he, did anyone else know what was happening?'

'A few, some of the wiser and more trusted types. His friends from the Argyll, people he'd grown up with, folks whose family had been here since early times. When things got really serious, he had to take them into his confidence.'

'But not his wife.'

'No. That's merely the way things were. I don't say it was right.'

'Okay. How did these people take it? Did they believe him?'

'But of course. Jack Bolding never lied, like I've already told you. As for your first question, people took the news very well. They rallied round and gave him useful, portable things he could carry round with him ready for the next trip to the other pace.'

'That sounds a bit cold blooded. What about sympathy?'

'Sympathy is cheap but help is help and it lasts longer.'

'Maybe, maybe but even so it was rather an incredible story to accept just like that.'

'Well, yes and no, because it wasn't the first time we'd heard of the other place.'

'No?'

'No. There've been stories about it before from time to time. Your grandfather would have told you about them if he'd lived long enough. Most of the old families around here know about the other place. Some of them have had people visit it, for there's a variety of means of entry. The 'Along-side Time' was the old name for it. I've heard it said that some people have lived out their lives there as either volunteers or conscripts like Bolding, though whether that's true or not I couldn't swear.'

'And that's where he is now?'

'I presume so. Who can say?'

'Did he just disappear, never to return?'

'No. I think he must have had a premonition that the next time he crossed over he wasn't coming back, because one particular night he came into the Argyll to say his farewells. He said that he'd already kissed his wife goodbye—not that she understood of course.'

'What did he say?'

'Not much. He stood us all a drink or two, for he didn't need money where he was going, and then he asked us to remember him from time to time, seeing as how our paths might be crossing although we'd not know it.'

'What did he mean?'

'Well think of it. We could be walking down a street here and in the other Binscombe, Jack might be strolling alongside us in the selfsame street at exactly the same time. It's possible we could even be occupying the same bit of space!

'Anyway, we wished him all the best and presented him with one of those Swiss army knives—very useful things, them—which we'd clubbed together to buy, anticipating such an event. We'd put a nice inscription to him on it and it had just about every tool conceivable so I thought we'd chosen well.'

'And then?'

'Well, that seemed to choke him a bit so he just said cheerio and left for home.'

'Never to be seen again.'

'That's right. Mind you, we leave a drink on his place at the bar in the Argyll every anniversary of that evening so as to remind us of him and just in case he comes back.'

'Do you think he ever will?'

'No, I don't suppose so. He's where he's meant to be.'

Conversation faltered as I harvested the weirdness in. It was an eerie thought. Bolding working away in his garden in Binscombe Crescent, all alone and surrounded by ruins and nature run wild while back here, in our Binscombe Crescent, a family lived out their normal life in the same spot. Then Disvan spoke again, raising suspicions that he'd been trespassing in my mind.

'Yes, curious concept isn't it?' he said. 'I often wonder if they ever catch a glimpse of his shadow or hear just a faint whisper of his gramophone playing. Perhaps he can sometimes sense some of their activities. Leastways, I hope that's so because it might be a comfort to him to know that life in his old home goes on. However, nothing of the kind has ever been reported to me.'

'Yes, I see. I suppose it depends on how close the two Binscombes are to each other, or maybe they even drift apart and then come together again in a cycle.'

'No one knows, Mr Oakley, although a lot of thought's been given to it. Not least by those who go there.'

Mr Disvan looked up and round and seemed lost in meditation for a considerable while. What I had just heard equally occupied my mind as I tried, with limited success, to reconcile its other-worldliness with the prosaic normality I saw all about me in the recreation ground. At length he broke the silence.

'Of course, to those who are aware of it, such knowledge breeds a kind of uncertainty. That's how I knew, right away before you said anything, that you had a close connection with here. It's passed on in the blood, and what's bred in the bone comes out in the meat. It shows in your manner even though you might know nothing about it.'

'What do you mean, "uncertainty"?'

'Well, consider Mr Oakley; there you are on a misty street, or turning a corner during a solitary walk, or waking in a darkened room, or even leaving your front door, and the question always arises. Which Binscombe am I in?'

Till Death Do Us Part

'It is rather good, though I say it myself,' said Mr Morton and even I, for all my ignorance of fish, had to share in the general admiration of the monster catch he'd brought in to the Argyll.

'How big is it?' said Mr Disvan.

'Just a touch over fifteen pounds.'

'I'll warrant that's an all time record catch for the lake.'

'Possibly, possibly,' replied Morton with characteristic modesty. 'The Club Captain thought it might be, but the old records will need to be checked before we can say for sure.'

Disvan was adamant. 'Take my word for it, Harry; that pike is the biggest ever caught in Broadwater or I'm a Dutchman.

'How about donating it to the Argyll?' said our host. 'I'd be prepared to have it stuffed and mounted in a frame, all nice like, with a bit of water weed in the background and a little plaque on the front.'

'I'd be happy to give it to you, just so long as the fishing club's name was given due prominence, of course. It's only because of the experience I've gained with them over the years that I was able to catch the fish.'

'Nonsense, Harry,' said the landlord, 'you're too self-effacing. You've forgotten more about fishing than that lot ever knew. Look at the way they stand out in the cold and rain for hours with not a minnow to show for it. Whereas you on the other hand—well,

I can't recall the last fishing trip you didn't bring in a whopper. When you're allowed to go, that is,' he added darkly.

Mr Morton steadfastly ignored this passing reference to Mrs Morton (who was well known to us all) although a brief shadow crossed his face.

'Yes, I think the fish would look nice in a case above the bar. Perhaps you should take it now and put it in your freezer.'

'Righto. I'll ring up the brewery tomorrow and see if they'll cough up the necessary. 'A sporting trophy,' I'll say, 'the displaying of which is intended to encourage the regular patronage of the local Angling Society.' You have to dangle increased profits in front of them before they'll sanction a new towel for the gents nowadays you see. It's the company accountants up in Reading to blame—never been in a public house in their lives I bet. Wine-bar types, more like it.'

The subject of brewery policy was one of the landlord's pet hobby-horses, one he could ride into a mad lathering gallop given a hint of encouragement. Accordingly no one spoke for a moment in order that a little blessed peace might settle. Mr Disvan, safe in his local authority, was the natural person to resume the conversation, and when he did so it was in order to steer us back to the uncontroversial subject of the silver white corpse before us—a being whose every passion was spent, whose hunger had been finally satisfied, and whose ears could no longer take offence.

'Pike specialist are you, Harry?'

Morton considered this, seeking as ever for the strictly truthful answer before replying.

'Only in a manner of speaking; I don't think there's a kind of native fish that I haven't gone for at some time or other but, yes, I like taking pike because there's an especial lot of thought and cunning involved.'

'What did you use to catch it?' asked someone.

Morton looked a little shamefaced. 'Ah... livebait, I'm afraid. A small gudgeon. It's sad, but that's the best way to do it.'

'Vicious looking brute, isn't he,' said the landlord.

'She, actually, but yes, they are vicious as we would see it, although they're just obeying their orders, so to speak.'

'Just obeying orders isn't a valid defence, Harry. Nuremberg War Trials 1945,' said Disvan.

'Well no, Mr Disvan, but that's with reference to Nazis, not fish. Fish have to do what the Almighty designed them to do, like it or not.'

'Perhaps,' said Disvan—refusing, however unreasonably, to relinquish the last word.

I sensed the start of one of the long, discursive and ultimately absurd dialogues peculiar to Binscombe people who saw nothing strange in debating Nazi fish or the ethics of aquatic life, but this one, sadly perhaps, died the death. Instead, conversation lingered fitfully in the realms of the material world.

'The pike used to be called 'the water wolf' you know,' said Mr Morton, 'seeing as it's so savage. In fact, some of the older anglers still call it that so as to keep in mind what they're trying to catch.'

'Is it true that they pull down ducklings?' said the landlord.

'Apparently, though I've never seen it done. They're quite capable of it and this one was certainly strong enough.'

'A sort of duck version of *Jaws*, eh, Harry?'

'What?'

'*Jaws*. A film.'

'Was it about fishing?'

'It doesn't matter.'

'This one's been around for years and years ruling the roost in Broadwater,' Morton continued, unworried by his lack of cinematic knowledge. 'She's been hooked before so we knew about her but up to now she's always managed to slip away.'

'Well,' said the landlord, putting his face down on a level with the fish's, 'that's an end to your little game. No more duckies for you.'

'In America,' said Morton, 'there's a species of pike called muskel-something which can be six foot in length.'

The Landlord continued his eyeball-to-eyeball gloat over the fish for only a few seconds more after receiving this intelligence. He withdrew his face and stood up.

'Well, even if you do have relatives taller than I am, it's still the end of your game.'

This reassertion of human supremacy might just as well have been directed to Mr Morton for, a few seconds after, the pub door crashed open and Mrs Morton not so much entered as boarded the premises.

'Where the hell have you been?' she shouted.

Harry looked around for support but found none. The group beside him melted away as if from one singled out by the finger of the Grim Reaper. Even the Landlord, whose home after all it was, suddenly found some urgent glass washing and bottle rearranging to do. Only Disvan, for reasons best known to himself, and I, a poor 'foreigner', stood by Morton, whose pallor was fast becoming as pale as that of the fish on the bar. Elsewhere, embarrassed conversations started as, out of the best of intentions, everyone pretended their minds were any place other than on Harry's humiliation.

'I said,' she continued from the open doorway, 'where the hell have you been?'

'Fishing,' Harry replied with a defiance in which not even the most generously inclined witness could detect conviction.

'And what—about—the—bloody—decorating, you stupid little man? Fish we can buy any time, but the house is where I have to live, damn it—in case you'd forgotten. Didn't I set this weekend aside for decorating?'

'Well you did, but...'

'So you go fishing.'

'It was a club match and I'd already promised...'

'Shut up.'

'But....'

'Come here.'

He did so, slowly perhaps and with an apology to each group of locals he passed, but come he did like a puppy to its bath. At length, upon his arrival at the door, Mrs Morton placed her formidable hand upon his back and propelled him through. At us, huddled together like a defeated tribe, she cast a leisurely glance that conveyed within it a degree of withering contempt worthy of a great actress. Then she made to sweep out when Disvan's commanding tones broke the silence.

'Mary Morton,' he said, pointing at her but without the least trace of anger in his voice, 'woman and girl I've known you, and you never were any good. You'll come to a bad end.'

I'd never heard Disvan directly rebuke anyone in this way before and in Binscombe terms it should have been the equivalent of excommunication and lifelong exile rolled into one.

For all the effect on Mrs Morton it might as well have been a sheep's growl. Eyes blazing with grim delight she wordlessly advanced, like the war machine of a science fiction epic, upon Disvan, stood before him a second, and then, with a gesture of disdain, flicked off his Panama hat.

The whole episode, from the moment of her entry, had seemed improper, and seeing Disvan, bareheaded and saddened, gazing at Mary Morton's retreating back, made it doubly so. Accordingly, as if by common consent, when the pub door slammed shut behind the female fighting fury, one and all acted as if nothing had occurred.

With considerable dignity, given the circumstances, Disvan retrieved his hat and resumed his place at the bar. The landlord now felt able to abandon his bottles and joined us once more.

'There goes a man who must envy the dead,' he said.

'Poor devil,' I replied. 'Why does he stand for it?'

'God knows.'

As ever, Disvan winced slightly at this cavalier attitude to the third commandment. 'Now, now,' he said, 'I'm sure she must have some redeeming features otherwise he wouldn't stay with her.'

'I wouldn't be so sure. It has to be said that although Morton's a very nice man, a very nice man indeed, he's also a fool and too weak to leave her. You know that she's off with other men, don't you?'

I raised my eyebrows in a gesture that committed me to no particular opinion and Disvan said, 'So they say,' in a tone that meant: yes, I do know and no, I don't approve of gossip.

'Flaunts it in his face she does, but still he don't do anything about it. Too weak and foolish.'

'Since when,' said Disvan, 'has a weakness of character made anyone a fool? It's just the way he was born.'

'Ah, well now you're getting back to the morals of fish and Nazi war crimes, and I'm afraid I'm not much of a one for philosophy.'

The landlord turned away, bringing a physical end to the conversation and pseudo-inquest on the distasteful incident which had preceded it. He took with him the monster pike which had lain on the bar throughout. On his way he raised it to his face level as if in conversation.

'It's all your fault,' he informed it.

* * *

'Oh yes. Horrible agony!'

Inhibitions loosened by barley wine, Doctor Bani-Sadr was regaling, if that is the right word, the assembled company in the Argyll with an account of Mrs Morton's sudden and tragic death.

'But how on earth did she come to eat a fish-hook, of all things?' said Mr Disvan.

'Because it was embedded in a fish she was eating at the time. It was an old, rusty hook that the fish must have swallowed whole at some point in the past and in the course of time it became enveloped in the flesh of the still living fish. It's an unusual process but not unknown.'

'Still, you'd think she'd have felt it in her mouth when she chewed the fish.'

'Did you ever see her eat?' said the landlord. ' "Guts", we used to call her at school, 'cause she'd put food down like it was going to be snatched away from her. A very distressing sight.'

'That's what I presume happened,' said the doctor. 'Anyway, by the time I was called and then the ambulance got her into hospital, half her insides were torn to shreds. Horrible agony as I said. Nothing we could do to save her—disembowelled from the inside, she was. Last time I saw anything that bad was a booby trap the Mau-Mau rigged up when I was doing my National Service. It did much the same to my colour-sergeant.'

'You said she'd come to a bad end, Mr Disvan,' said the landlord.

'I wasn't prophesying when I said it,' he replied, 'and I wouldn't wish what happened to her on anyone.'

'Ay-up!'

This sotto voce warning came from someone who chanced to be facing the door while the above exchange went on. We instinctively quietened and looked cautiously round to see that Mr Morton had entered the bar. He was dressed in a dark suit with black armbands attached with clumsy stitches and he seemed as genuinely sombre as his attire.

'Good morning, Mr Disvan, Doctor Bani-Sadr, gentlemen.'

'Hello there, Harry,' said the landlord. 'Is there anything I can get you?'

'No, thank you kindly, I've got to be at the funeral shortly. I just popped in to say a general thank you to you all for the card and words of commiseration I've received. Perhaps I might see a few of you at the service. You'd be very welcome.'

There was a polite non-committal rumble in response to this invitation and the proprieties thus being served, Morton took his leave.

'Is anyone going?' asked our host.

'Not I,' said someone.

'The only reason I'd go is to make damn sure she goes under,' said another of obviously similar opinion.

'We all clubbed together to send a wreath,' rejoined the first, 'to show a bit of respect for Harry. Why go any further and make hypocrites of ourselves?'

'Still, someone ought to go, to represent the village. How about you, Mr Disvan?'

'Very well, I'll go, even though she never bore any love for me.'

'When did she ever bear any love for anyone in her life?' said the man who'd criticised her before.

The landlord leaned forward and whispered conspiratorially in my ear, 'She led him a terrible dance when he was a youngster, enticed him on and then jilted him. That's why he's so bitter.'

'Well, when you've all finished speaking ill of the dead,' announced Mr Disvan, 'I still think there ought to be a village contingent, however small, at the interring. Will you accompany me, Mr Oakley?'

I had felt a guilty twinge of sympathy for the friendless Mary Morton and so said that I would.

'So will I,' said Doctor Bani-Sadr. 'Since I both delivered her and was there when she died, I might as well see the story through.'

'Three of you, that'll do,' said the landlord. 'Mind you, you'd best be off in a minute if you're to catch the service.'

'Let's not take things too far,' said Mr Disvan. 'Remember who we're talking about. It'll be enough if we're present at the graveside afterwards. Your round I believe, Mr Oakley?'

* * *

At length Mr Disvan consulted his digital watch and said we should be going. The church was a mere half mile away and so we set off on foot at an easy pace through the intent grouplets of Saturday shoppers.

'So you were there when she died were you, doctor?' said Mr Disvan.

'I was. One of the most harrowing deaths I've seen in forty years of medical practise, I might add.'

'Because of the pain she was in?' I tentatively

48

suggested.

'Well no... not entirely.'

Mr Disvan's tone was far more definite. 'No. Because of what she said.'

Doctor Bani-Sadr stopped in his tracks and stared at Disvan with mixed suspicion and curiosity. A group of ladies who'd been half-heartedly inspecting a greengrocer's window display turned to regard our little drama.

'How did you know?' said the Doctor.

'I didn't,' Disvan replied. 'It just seemed unlikely that Mary Morton would leave the world behind without a parting shot—at poor old Harry I suppose.'

Bani-Sadr seemed placated by this response. 'Ah I see. Well, as long as it's only deduction you're using this time that's okay.'

This seemed the sort of statement that was worth following up in the hope of obtaining precious information about the Disvan phenomenon but now was neither the time or the place.

Seeing that nothing violent or interesting would come of our little debate the women turned back slowly to their scrutiny of fruit and veg.

We went on our way as before.

'Do you want to know what she said?'

'Only if you want to tell us.'

Bani-Sadr considered this for a small while.

'Yes I think I do although I'm not clear as to why. In the normal course of things doctors have to keep a lot of secrets.'

'Well, just as you wish.'

'Just between us, mind you—oh, and you too of course, Mr Oakley—but no further.'

'You have our word,' said Disvan speaking for me (albeit correctly) as he did distressingly often.

'What appalled me, you see, was the bitterness.

I've never seen such an intensity of bitterness and malevolence—not just at her husband, although he got the brunt, but also at the nurses, the world, the universe. She was willing to take them all on.'

'That was her great strength, if you can call it that,' Disvan concurred.

'Well she certainly had strength from some source or other, but in the end it didn't do her any good. Quite the opposite, in fact, for it made her agony long and drawn out. We were just applying more powerful sedatives and getting ready to operate when she surged out of the doze we'd managed to get her in and sat up straight on the table—something she shouldn't have been able to do with all the damage sustained and all the drugs she'd got in her. Anyway, possible or not, she sat up and grabbed Harry by the lapels—we'd brought him in since she was likely to go at any moment—and dragged him towards her so they were eyeball to eyeball. "Don't think I'm going to let you go fishing!" she shouted and then fell back. Dead.'

'Sounds a ghastly scene,' I said, visualising it all too clearly.

'You don't know the half of it. Even when she was gone we still had a struggle with her. She'd gripped Harry's lapels so tight it took two nurses and the anaesthetist to prise her fists open so he could get away. By that time poor old Harry was in a fine old state. Imagine it, your wife's last words being a threat. And a vicious, empty one at that.'

Curiosity overcame my better judgement and, just as we drew near the church, I could not forbear to ask something that had been preying on my mind since I heard of Mrs Morton's death.

'Between us, do you think that... I mean, is it possible that Harry...'

'That Harry what?' said Disvan seemingly non-plussed.

'Well, given the way in which she died and what caused it, you know... a fishing hook.'

Enlightenment clearly dawned on Disvan's face.

'You mean did Harry murder her?'

His voice was loud enough to attract the attention of several passers-by and I keenly avoided their ensuing scrutiny.

'Well yes, that's what I do mean.'

'Put your mind at rest, Mr Oakley,' said Disvan as Doctor Bani-Sadr nodded firmly in agreement, 'the only thing Harry has ever hurt or ever could hurt is a fish or the maggots he uses to catch them. The fact that it was a fish hook of all things that took Mary Morton away is just one of the proofs that the Almighty has a sense of humour.'

* * *

The funeral was a wretched affair. Shamefully few people issued from the church after the memorial service to join us by the graveside. Aside from us three, only her husband, a distant and aged relative (whom we later learned was very keen on such services) and the priest were there to see Mary Morton off on her final journey.

Father Wiltshire was well aware of the nature of the person he was burying, but with the Christian charity and easy-going nature for which he was well known, he still managed to put a depth of feeling into his words. I, alas, could muster no such creditable sentiments and so began to study the people gathered together for this inadequate peace-making with death.

The elderly, distant relative seemed unaware of

her surroundings and looked blankly to a horizon personal to herself. I speculated that she was travelling down the years and reviewing the other, more grievous, funerals she had doubtless known.

Doctor Bani-Sadr, who was well known to be a free thinker or even pagan, ignored the priest's words and allowed his gaze to range widely from the undertaker's bearers waiting patiently by with the coffin, to the heads of vaguely curious passers-by visible over the churchyard wall and then back to the grave which yawned to take Mary's remains into eternity.

Mr Disvan appeared, for all I could tell, to be listening to Father Wiltshire's words of comfort and consolation but where his thoughts ranged, as always, I could not discern.

At length I looked at Harry Morton and was shocked to see that, even more than the doctor, he was paying no attention to the service. His rapt attention was fixed beyond us, on the glint, just visible between the churchyard yew trees, of Broadwater Lake. Meanwhile, presumably unbeknown to himself, his hands made a reeling motion as he played an imaginary fish.

* * *

'Long time no see, Harry,' said the landlord. 'How are you finding the single life ?'

'Very well, thank you.'

'What'll you have?'

'A rum and Coca-Cola, I think, please.'

'What? Not the usual half of mild?'

'No, not today. I fancy a rum and coke.'

'Large or small?'

'Large, certainly.'

'Coming straight up.'

'Been doing much fishing?' I asked innocently, clearly remembering the scene by the graveside even though several months had since passed.

'No. I thought I should observe a period of mourning as a mark of respect to poor Mary.'

'I see.'

'But of course one can't go mourning for ever,' he continued eagerly, 'and it's about fishing that I've come to see you all.'

'What do you mean?' asked Disvan.

'Well, what I had in mind was a fishing expedition down to the coast. I could organise a boat for each day and lodgings in a bed and breakfast place. We could take beer and sandwiches out with us when we're fishing and then go and visit the bright lights when we're not.'

'Sounds fine,' said Disvan. 'You say you'd organise it?'

'Yes, start to finish.'

'How will you find the time?'

'That's the least of my worries, I've got plenty of time nowadays.'

'We thought you were decorating the house, inside and out,' said the landlord.

'Oh, that can wait. It'll still be there when we get back.'

'Not all of us have rods.'

'I've got a number of spare ones all ready to use. I've been using my leisure to overhaul my fishing tackle, you see, so it's all in tip-top condition and raring to go. If we need anything more I'll hire it.'

'Well you seem to have it all thought out, Harry,' Mr Disvan commented, seemingly impressed.

'I have. What about you, Mr Oakley, I take it you'll be joining us?'

'But I don't fish.'

'Doesn't matter. You can always learn or just come along for the beer and company.'

'But...'

'No buts please, Mr Oakley, you come along and you'll thank me for it afterwards.'

'Well, okay then.'

'Good. Right, I'll make a list of the rest.'

And so it was that, within the space of ten minutes, the transformed and forceful Harry Morton had signed most of us up in his little venture and even extracted deposit money from many. The landlord had agreed to supply quantities of bottled beer as his contribution to the jaunt and others had promised to bring provisions.

'Right then, that's all settled. I'll see about the boat and accommodation for the weekend and I'll fix up a mini-bus to get us there. We'll meet outside the Argyll, 7 o'clock sharp Friday evening, okay?'

A ragged chorus of yes sort of noises answered this and, thus placated, Harry took both himself and his optimistic bustling energy out of the pub.

'Was that Harry Morton, or an engaging impostor?' asked the landlord.

'It was a post-liberation-of-the-slaves Harry,' said someone.

'A walking advertisement for bereavement,' said another.

'I'm told that when the life assurance people pay up he'll be quite well off,' a third chipped in.

The landlord smiled benevolently. 'Life, I'd like you to meet Harry Morton. Harry Morton, meet Life. I hope you'll get on together.'

* * *

In the event, Mr Morton's arrangements for the week-end trip were faultless. Our party was conveyed by the promised mini-bus to Coast Lodge, a beach-side boarding house of quite unreasonable comfort and friendliness. We went *en masse,* after an excellent tea, to inspect the craft Harry had hired for us and within an hour of our arrival by the sea we were venturing forth upon it. The owners of the guest house, a big-built man and his attractive wife came down to the beach with their two dogs to wave us off. Even the weather seemed willing to add its blessing to Mr Morton's brain child and granted us a warm, clear and still evening. In due course the stars came out and those of us who were not fishing, myself included, could give our full attention to the marvellous display they provided.

It was, I decided, an idyllic setting. We had moored perhaps a mile offshore at a point equidistant from the silent bright lights of Hastings on one side and Eastbourne on the other. Behind us were scattered points of yellow light marking the position of Pevensey and Pevensey Bay and I looked, without success, to see if I could make out the dark bulk of the hybrid Romano-Norman castle that we had passed in the bus earlier on.

A relaxed and contented quiet had settled over us after the initial attack on the supplies brought from home, and fishermen and observers alike seemed happily lost in their thoughts. The gentle lapping of the sea upon the boat and shore saved the silence from seeming unnatural.

Mr Disvan had produced a large meerschaum pipe from somewhere and was looking out over the sea while he smoked it. This surprised me on two counts for, in the first place, I had never seen him smoke before, and secondly because the smoke, when it reached me, was aromatic and sweet and entirely unlike that of normal tobacco. I tried to place where I'd encountered that herbal smell before and realised quickly that it was in the context of the concerts and student bed-sits of my early university days. I was wondering just how to frame the question that naturally sprang to mind when Mr Disvan saved me the trouble by addressing me:

'Looking for the castle are you, Mr Oakley?'

'Well, I was a moment ago, yes.'

'You won't be able to see it; there are no lights there at all—but that's the direction you'd need to look in.'

He indicated with his finger the general line of sight.

'A very interesting place, that,' he continued. 'Probably the last organised centre of resistance against the invaders in the Wealden area.'

'What invaders?'

'You lot. The Angles and Saxons and Jutes of course.'

'Oh, you're talking of way back, are you. Yes, I understand now.'

'In Roman times it was a port with its own squadron of war ships and a garrison of professional fighting men. Then when the Roman ways began to fail, I suppose people turned to it for guidance and protection.'

'But without success, presumably.'

'That's right. Time moves on, you see, and their particular time was over. There's little point in fighting against it although people persevere in doing so. However, while it lasted and there were men to man the walls, Pevensey Castle would have been the focal point of this stretch of coast. The last flickering light of Roman civilisation you might say, if you were feeling poetic.'

With this thought he lapsed into silence again leaving me to contemplate Roman Britain's last stand. I was just succeeding in visualising these stoic, doomed defenders (it was hard to imagine them without togas and legionary armour) when Disvan again broke my train of thought.

'Actually I'm misleading you to a certain extent,' he said absently. 'In those times the Castle wasn't a castle but what you might more properly call a fort, and its name was Anderida, not Pevensey. Similarly, I very much doubt that the men who held it were what we would understand as soldiers. A very late Roman document mentions a unit of barbarian mercenaries there.'

'You're very knowledgeable about all this.'

'So I should be.'

'What do you mean by that?'

'Nothing.'

He puffed away at his pipe, perhaps just the hint of a satisfied grin on his face at this drawing out of my restrained curiosity.

'So what happened?'

'They all died. The Anglo-Saxon Chronicle says that in 491 AD, and I quote: "Aelle and Cissa besieged Andredes Ceaster and slew all who were in there. Not one Briton was left alive".'

'You've been genning up on this specially for the trip.'

'No, I promise you not.'

'And with them, I suppose, went the last memory of Rome in the region.'

'Possibly not, but what does it matter? The invaders prevailed and we're a whole civilisation away from the events of that time. People should forget.'

This puzzled and intrigued me. 'Forget? I thought they had. Come on, out with it for once, Mr Disvan, what exactly do you mean?'

He looked relaxedly at me for a while and then opened his mouth to speak when, just at that moment, Harry let out a loud excited cry. Our attention was naturally diverted, and I thus never learnt the nature of Disvan's intended reply.

'What is it, Harry?' said someone.

'It's a catch, a catch,' he replied excitedly. 'My first in three months!'

'Good on you, boy,' said the landlord, 'bring 'er on in.'

Morton needed little urging; he played the fish like the natural he was, alternately feeding the line out and then feverishly reeling the victim in to its doom.

'A big-un is it, Harry?' said the off-duty Binscombe Community Policeman who was along with us.

'Moderate. Nothing enormous, but quite promising.'

'Well come on then, let's have a look at it.'

'I've nearly got it, she's weakening.' Harry pulled the rod almost vertical and reeled hard. 'Here we go!'

As these words escaped his lips, the water at the boat's edge erupted and from the water spout a large white figure surged with blinding speed to grasp Morton's fishing rod.

Harry screamed (it's possible that we all did) and attempted to retreat, but his collar was quickly grasped by an implacable strong arm. As we all cravenly drew back and abandoned him to his fate, Morton was gradually drawn to the boat's rail until his knees were hard against it and he had to fight to stop himself being dragged over.

What was once Mary Morton was considerably the worst for wear but still instantly recognisable as the woman we had known. With one arm over the rail and the other clasped like a lover's around Harry's neck, she stared with sightless eyes into her husband's terrified face while drawing him, slowly but surely, towards her. As he came she mouthed angry words and phrases at him but no sound came forth from the badly damaged throat.

Sensing the inevitable end to this unequal struggle, Harry recovered a modicum of self control and turned to face us:

'Help me, please, she's going to kill me!'

Mr Disvan stepped forward and shouted something that I either didn't quite catch or that was in a language I didn't understand. It seemed to have some effect because the monster woman turned to look at us for the first time.

Being under the relentless scrutiny of that dead, white face made me forget Harry's plight for a moment and wish with all my heart that Disvan had not attracted her attention. Fortunately (for us) the experience was not prolonged, for she shook her green matted hair and with a controlled, almost languid, motion spat contemptuously at Disvan before returning to her grisly endeavours.

She tightened her embrace and drew Harry right up to her waterlogged, naked body. Then, with a final heave, our friend's feet were lifted completely off the deck and the one-time husband and wife fell back into the water.

Even then, it seemed, the battle continued, for vigorous splashing noises could be heard interspersed with occasional desperate cries and, perhaps inspired or shamed by Morton's tenacious fight for life, I shook off my paralysis and rushed to help.

Quite what I intended to do remains unclear to this day, but en route to the point of Harry's departure I grabbed a boat hook, possibly with vain hopes of killing what was already dead.

Wielding this inadequate weapon I leaned, perhaps foolishly, over the side and instantly found myself face to face with the woman I'd seen buried a few months before. She was half raised out of the sea as, with both of her hands on the top of his head, she pushed her spouse beneath the waves. All that was visible of Harry was his pate and two wildly flailing arms. Realising that she was observed, the creature looked at me and grinned in triumph. For a mere second or so we exchanged glances as she went about her work. What Mary Morton saw in my face I cannot guess nor wish to speculate but for my part I recall only her white, water-filled eyeballs and the complete absence of earthly life behind them. It was a sight that will accompany me, ever fresh, till I at last reach my own grave.

Weakly and, I was later told, in a state of some shock, I fell back.

Our last sight of Harry Morton was of him being borne away, seemingly still alive, with his head clamped firmly under one of his wife's arms while the other propelled them strongly out to sea. A final despairing yell wafted back to us and then the gloom swallowed them up.

For several long minutes silence reigned on the boat before the constable aboard felt it his duty to try and rally us.

'He fell overboard,' he stated authoritatively. 'He accidentally fell overboard and for some inexplicable reason went down like a stone. That's what we'll say. What with both me and Mr Disvan testifying, no suspicion will fall upon us.'

'You can't be serious!' I interjected rather loudly. 'You saw what happened to Harry and you'll just say he fell overboard?'

'It's for the best, Mr Oakley,' said the landlord gently.

'After all,' agreed another, 'in a manner of speaking, that's what did happen. He did fall overboard. We don't have to say how exactly, do we?'

'Look at it this way, Mr Oakley,' said Disvan in as kindly a voice as I'd yet heard him use, 'what else could you say? Nobody would believe you, and getting yourself into a mess in that way won't bring Harry back, will it?'

Once considered, Disvan's argument seemed un-answerable, but even so a wave of bitterness at Morton's fate and the world in general swept over me.

'Whatever happened to the truth, Mr Disvan?'

'It lost credibility Mr Oakley, and went into hiding.'

'Amen,' said the policeman. 'Put the boat about. Let's head for home.'

* * *

Mr Morton's body was washed ashore several days later, 'slightly bashed about and nibbled by the fishes,' as the blunt and thick-skinned coastguard told Mr Disvan on the telephone.

After the legal formalities of autopsy and inquest were served, it therefore fell upon us to attend a second and final Morton funeral within the space of a few months. In contrast, however, to the previous occasion, a sizeable crowd of sincere mourners were present at the obsequies and people were arrayed two or three deep around the graveside.

To my horror I saw that it was intended to bury Harry in a double grave with his late wife, and I whispered to Mr Disvan who was beside me.

'This is appalling. Can't we do something to pre-vent it?'

'On what grounds, Mr Oakley?' he answered with a shrug.

Once again, as soon as I gave it more than cursory thought, any mention of the truth became obviously impossible.

'What I don't understand,' I continued quietly, 'is how she followed us there. I mean, was she physically there? Did she walk all that way travelling by night maybe? How did she know where we were?'

'The ways of the departed are not like ours, Mr Oakley. They see different things and are subject to different rules.'

'My God!' I said suddenly—and too loudly, for Father Wiltshire looked up and gave me a reproving glance. 'Look, the soil on her grave is all disturbed and churned up. She's been out of there!'

Disvan attempted to calm me. 'Not necessarily. The earth on her grave hasn't had time to settle properly yet, and the digging of Harry's trench would have disturbed hers anyway.'

I remained unplacated, however. 'Will she rest now, do you think?'

'Yes, I would imagine so, Mr Oakley. She got her own way in the end. Harry was made to do as he was told and that was all that ever really mattered to her. He's back in her power now, so perhaps she'll be satisfied.'

I fell silent and the sun seemed to lose its warmth as I pondered how Mary Morton had spent the hours after leaving our world behind, and by what long weary roads she had travelled to the sea and her moment of victory.

While I was thus lost in thought, the policeman edged his way over to us and discreetly sought our attention.

'You seem out of sorts, Mr Oakley.'

Mr Disvan answered for me. 'I believe he is, Stan.'

'And would I be right in saying it's because you

think that the Morton woman's finally won?'

'Yes,' I said, 'you would be right.'

'There you are then! Can I tell him, Mr Disvan?'

Disvan mused for a moment and then nodded his head. The constable turned animatedly to me and whispered in my ear.

'She's not going to win. Harry is—finally and conclusively and in a fitting manner. We're not leaving Harry to spend eternity alongside her. We're going to weigh her down in death the way she weighed Harry down in life, and we're going to feed her to Harry's beloved fish in Broadwater Lake.'

'What on earth do you mean?'

He looked left and right before replying, as if he feared eavesdroppers, even though all those present were well disposed Binscombe folk.

'What I mean, Mr Oakley, is an unofficial midnight exhumation party. Are you with us?'

I looked at Mr Disvan for confirmation of what I thought I'd heard. He coolly returned my gaze from the edge of his eyes.

'It seems reasonable, Mr Oakley,' he said. 'She forbade Harry to go fishing and Providence appears prepared to let that be enforced, even from beyond the grave. However, nothing was said that she shouldn't await judgement day sleeping with the fishes.'

Only One Careful Owner

'Good wood, Albert,' cried someone as Mr Whiteburgh's bowl gently kissed the side of the jack on its way past, thereby making the ultimate victory of the Binscombe team seem all the more certain.

Less demonstrative, but just as enthusiastic, Mr Disvan joined with the round of appreciative applause.

'They'll not catch us now,' he confided to me.

The home Goldenford side appeared to share this view and started to relax the frightening degree of concentration they always brought to this local derby. A few of them went so far as to strike up easygoing conversations with their opponents, probably about the drinking which normally followed the game, and the events of the year since the last one.

Although I would not have admitted it in present company, I was relatively indifferent to the match's outcome. My motives for attending had more to do with the idyllic setting and attendant jollities than any burning desire to witness victory. Someone who was observing me rather than the game would have noticed that, for the most part, my attention was devoted to the river which flowed beside the bowling green and to the boggy Lammas lands beyond. For all my years of residence, I had yet to find in myself the professed and fervid Binscombe patriotism of my circle of friends.

The church clock struck seven. The sun was just setting over its Norman tower and casting a friendly if waning light over the raised ground of the graveyard. Mr Disvan had told me that the vast yews which stood within it had, in their comparative youth, probably provided longbows for the battles of the Hundred Years War. I'd read elsewhere, however, that the best bow staves had been generally imported from Spain. Even so, it was a pleasing notion and so I had kept my sceptical modern theories to myself.

It seemed to me that the setting could be part of a 'This England' calendar scene, and I one of the anonymous archetypal Englishmen within it.

As very often happened, no sooner had any halfway agreeable idea entered my head than the world somehow instantly intruded to blow the concept asunder. In this particular instance, the world's emissary was the screech of car brakes and the repeated sounding of a horn.

Everyone looked up to see that a yellow Ford Fiesta had come to a halt, quite illegally it should be said, on the road that ran parallel to the river and the associated recreation grounds. The highway was some way off and so the owner of the offending vehicle could not be made out.

'Anyone recognise it?' said the Goldenford Captain, a burly red-faced man with arms like giant hams. Nobody did and so the game continued.

Obviously frustrated by our lack of response to his signals, the motorist left his car and set off towards us on foot. Another figure, a female one, similarly alighted and followed on at a lesser pace. It seemed their intentions were friendly, for the young man in the lead was waving at us.

'I know who it is,' said Mr Disvan, squinting at the approaching visitors. 'It's Trevor Jones and his young lady.'

'Who are they?' I inquired.

'Don't you know them? They're both Binscombe

people. Their families have been around here for a long, long time.'

'I don't recall the name.'

'Possibly not. They've both been away at university so you may have missed meeting them.'

'I see.'

'We're very proud of them. As far as I know, they're the first Binscombe youngsters to go to university, apart from the Tamlyn boy who went to theological college, which isn't quite the same thing—and the Binscombe Scholarship, of course, but that's another story. Also, they started courting before they went away, so they've done well to stay together all that time, given the temptations and distractions.'

'I suppose they have.'

By this time the young couple were almost upon us. Close to, I now recognised them as people I'd seen very occasionally, although never to speak to. The young man, Trevor, as I now knew him to be, appeared bright and personable even if his taste in clothes ran to the somewhat garish. His 'young lady', as Mr Disvan quaintly termed her, was as dark haired and dark complexioned as her boyfriend was fair, and seemed as quietly demure as he, by all tokens so far, was not.

Jones sauntered up, a broad relaxed smile on his face.

'Hello, everyone. Mr Disvan, how are you?'

The men of Goldenford were not used to even such a mild manifestation of eccentricity as this and looked to Disvan for guidance. Should the stranger be dealt with, or could the game continue?

'It's okay,' Mr Disvan announced, 'he's known to us.'

Jones seemed genuinely amazed that anyone should doubt this. 'That's right,' he said, 'carry on.'

And, with perhaps the merest tokens of disbelief, this they did.

Young Trevor shook hands with Disvan and was then introduced to me. As eve,r the seemingly irrelevant point of my family's ancient links with Binscombe was brought up in the same breath as my name. The young lady turned out to be called Tania, Tania Knott, although the apparent intention was that her name should soon become Jones as well. Whereas Trevor's greeting to me was amiability itself, it struck me that her words of introduction betokened more human warmth behind them.

'So you're back from university, are you?' said Mr Wessner, our 'man from the Town Hall', stating the obvious as a conversational gambit.

'Yes,' Trevor smiled, 'we're finished there now. The results will be out in a month or so and then we'll know whether we've wasted the last three years or not.'

'We've every confidence in you,' said Mr Disvan. 'I'm sure you'll do well in your exams.'

Trevor smiled knowingly at Tania. 'Let's hope your faith isn't misplaced' he said.

'What subject did you read?' I asked.

'Electrical engineering; we both did.'

'Oh, that's interesting because—'

Mr Disvan closed off this avenue of inquiry by interrupting. 'And what are you up to at the moment?'

'Decorating mostly, in between writing job applications. As you know, Tania's father gave us a place in Quarry Lane as an advance wedding present and it needs quite a bit of work doing on it.'

'Yes,' said Disvan, 'I know the place. It used to belong to a couple called Bellingham, Jehovah's Witnesses as I recall. When the wife died, old man Bellingham lost interest in things, religion included, and let the house and garden go rather.'

'Anyway,' said Trevor, 'that's all getting away from why I came over to see you. I wanted you all to see our car.'

'You've bought a car?' said the landlord who was with us.

'Yep, our first. We got it today.'

'We've just driven it back from the car auction,' added Tania. 'It seems very nice. Come and have a look.'

Since the game's conclusion now seemed forgone, the Binscombe spectators, a dozen or so in all, duly did as they were bidden and we trooped up over the recreation ground and through the children's swings to the double-yellow-lined roadside.

'Isn't it a little bit dodgy to buy from motor auctions if you're not in the trade?' asked Mr Wessner, whom life and experience had made a pessimist.

'Sometimes,' replied Trevor, nothing daunted, 'but Tarn and I are pretty good with machines and we gave it a thorough going over before buying. As far as I can make out it's as sound as a bell.'

'The dealer said it'd only had one careful owner,' Tania said.

A few covertly smiled at this, but no one was impolite enough to voice their cynical views. Mr Patel said that his brother, the one from Winchester, had had one of those cars once and he'd been full of praise for it till he wrote it off on the M25.

Still consumed with pride at his acquisition, despite this last hint of mortality, Trevor got in and revved the motor for us. Then he invited us to inspect the engine and we, instant experts all, made obliging approval noises at its tone and appearance.

'Well then,' he said by way of summation, 'what do you think?'

We all agreed it was 'very nice'.

Obviously pleased with this, a further idea struck the young man. 'Tarn, how about a picture?'

Miss Knott looked into the depths of her bright red bag and brought forth a little camera.

'Would you oblige, Mr Disvan?'

'Not I, I'm afraid,' he replied. 'I've no facility with such things. You'd come out minus your heads or feet.'

'How about you, Mr Oakley, then?'

'Okay.'

Accordingly an informal study of the car and its proud owners was taken. It was a quite pleasing shot with the young couple arm in arm beside the vehicle, with the church and sunset as a backdrop. My only anxiety was that there might not be enough light.

The moment and their pleasure thus captured for all time the Jones-to-be bid us farewell and sped off. Us older folk, probably all engrossed in our own memories of youth, slowly returned to the dying stages of the bowls match and the celebrations to follow.

* * *

'Hang on—who's the little girl?' said the landlord holding the photograph aloft.

'You may well ask,' replied Trevor, an unbecoming pensive look on his face.

The assembled company formed a jostling semi-circle around the bar seeking a view of the picture the young couple had brought in. A certain respectful space was left for Mr Disvan and, since I was beside him, I was able to gain a relatively clear view.

My fears about lack of light had been unjustified. In technical and aesthetic terms the picture was faultless. The car featured well and the couple's shared pleasure in life was evident from their easy pose and unforced smiles. The church spire and golden red glow of the sky added a touch of timelessness to the human event that the picture celebrated. All of this however went unnoticed and unappreciated, because clearly visible in the back seat of the car was a little flaxen-haired girl.

The fact that her presence there was unaccountable may have had something to do with it, but it seemed to me that her face, partly turned towards the camera and partly hidden in shadow, was not regarding us in any friendly fashion.

'It's a trick of the light,' said the landlord. 'Here, have a drink on the house.'

Tania accepted the proffered brandy with thanks. 'Do you really think so?' she said. 'It seems an awfully clear image.'

'It must be. What else could it be?'

A silence fell as everyone pondered possible answers to this rhetorical question.

'Perhaps there's something wrong with your camera,' suggested Mr Disvan. 'Were the other pictures on that film all right?'

Trevor flicked rapidly through the rest of the photographs in the yellow envelope he held. 'As far as we can see, yes, they're all perfectly normal. There's one taken on our holiday in Spain, some from the trip out to Basing House; all sorts of lighting and conditions, but they're all okay.'

'Maybe the camera was fed up with just seeing you two and decided to add someone to the last picture for variety's sake,' said Mr Wessner, in a rare stab at humour.

Trevor glared at him. 'It isn't funny. Seeing this has put Tania right off the car.'

One did not need any great powers of insight to observe that his fiancée was not the only person thus unnerved.

'Here,' said the landlord, taking the photograph and passing it round, 'does anyone recognise her?'

The picture was duly exchanged from hand to hand and each person more or less gingerly inspected the girl who should not be there. No one thought that her face was familiar.

When the picture reached me I saw that the image of the intruding cuckoo-in-the-nest was hard edged and well defined, unlike any of the other photographic oddities I'd seen from time to time. Lines of the car's interior shape disappeared out of sight behind the figure as they would do with a real person. The shadows which partly covered her and mercifully hid half of her face consistently affected the surroundings as well.

At present our technology can record events, but not the emotions which accompanied them. To me, however, this photograph somehow made the necessary leap into the far future and faithfully evoked a sense of malevolence that had come unbidden into what should have been a happy scene. From the various expressions of my fellow patrons in the Argyll I could see that I was not alone in feeling this.

'Of course it's a trick of the light,' the landlord continued. 'It's something to do with the peculiar effects of the sunset, I expect.'

He smiled reassuringly at the young couple but though they mustered a friendly expression in return it was plain that they were unconvinced.

'Look,' he said, 'I'll prove it to you. Lottie, go and get the camera please. The rest of you follow me.'

His wife went off to do as she was asked and we all obediently shambled after him as he came round the bar and headed for the door.

'What are you going to do?' asked Trevor.

'I should have thought that was obvious,' the landlord replied. 'If there is something in the car then it'll show up again. If there isn't and it was just a one-off freak effect, then all a photo will show is a car. Simple as that, isn't it? I've got a Polaroid so we'll know straight away. Where's Lottie got to?'

The landlady came forward and gave him the camera. We all assembled in the pub forecourt and congregated in a circle round the Jones's car. Passers-by, commuters home from London, looked furtively at this strange gathering in a car park but did not slow their onward rush in order to see its outcome.

'People hurry their lives away, don't they,' said Mr Disvan observing them sadly.

'Sunday drinkers,' remarked the landlord in a disparaging tone concurring, as always, with Disvan. 'Anyway, never mind them; let's get this business sorted out.'

He whipped the camera to his face and snapped off a rapid picture in the car's general direction. A few seconds later the print began to emerge slowly from the camera's base.

'You've got to allow a minute or so for it to develop. Keep your fingers crossed.'

An air of anticipation grew as we looked from camera to car and back again, all of us doubtless wondering if an unseen passenger in the car was similarly observing us. This thought provoked uncomfortable sensations and silence fell. Trevor and Tania exchanged hopeful glances, although the former tried to appear reassuringly confident.

At last the landlord ripped off the black protective covering from the picture and scrutinised it closely. Instantly his jaw sagged and his eyes widened. 'Oh my God,' he said. 'Oh no!'

'What is it? What is it?' shouted Trevor. Tania looked sidelong and fearfully at the car.

'Nothing, just a picture of a car,' said the landlord, smiling and in his normal voice now. 'I was just having you on. See for yourself.'

Trevor almost snatched the photograph from him and gave it his undivided attention. A smile then similarly spread across his face and the still sticky picture was passed around the group. As the landlord had said, all it showed was an unremarkable, quite unoccupied yellow Ford Fiesta.

'Praise be,' said Tania.

'A trick of the light, like I said,' the landlord concluded, pleased with the obvious triumph of his theory. 'Look, I'll prove it to you further. Someone go and get Lenin from behind the bar.'

Mr Disvan, who liked animals, went to fetch said Alsatian and soon returned with him trotting obediently by his side.

'Okay,' our master of ceremonies continued, 'now, as you all know, it's said that dumb animals can sense wrongness and see things that we don't see. Is that not so, Mr Disvan?'

'It is so said,' Disvan replied.

'Well then, young Trevor, with your permission we'll try and get Lenin to sit in the back seat of the car. If there's something nasty there he'll refuse or growl or do some such thing, won't he?'

Trevor, torn between his electrical engineering world into which such beliefs did not intrude and his desire for undisputed ownership of his car, mumbled vague agreement.

'Right, let's go. Come on, Lenin, in you go, there's a good boy.'

Trevor unlocked and held the door open for the

huge dog while the landlord ushered it in.

Lenin, although perhaps a little puzzled, did not hesitate at all. With one bound he was seated in the back of the car, huffing happily away at his master in anticipation of what would happen next in this game.

'That concludes that, then,' said the landlord.

We all smiled in relief, already beginning to revise the episode in our minds so as to minimise the seriousness with which we had treated it.

'Poor old Lenin doesn't understand what's going on, do you, boy?' said Lottie the landlady, for the dog was looking perplexedly from face to face, waiting for the next development. 'He does look funny sitting there. I think I'll take a picture.'

This she duly did.

The crowd started to wander back to the Argyll while Trevor lingered behind to lock up his car. Lenin, pleased to have been of service even if he didn't know how, walked jauntily by the landlord's heels, tail wagging hard. Suddenly, just as Mr Patel in the lead placed his hand on the door to enter the bar, a piercing female scream from behind brought our progress to a halt.

The landlady was standing aghast, staring at a picture held in both hands. The camera, broken and unregarded, lay where she had dropped on the ground.

'Oh, my Lord,' she said, 'she's there. She's got her arm around Lenin and... and she's baring her teeth at us!'

* * *

'It took me weeks and weeks to persuade Tania to ride in the car again after that second photograph, and now this happens!' said Trevor, leaning dejectedly against the bar.

'You mean you managed to explain that picture away?' said the landlord.

'No, not really, it's just that with the passage of time she got over the shock and let it fade from her mind.'

'It shan't fade from my mind, I can assure you,' said Lottie. 'There's something evil about the whole business.'

'Probably, probably,' Trevor replied, waving a placatory hand at her, 'but just please don't say such things when Tania is about.'

'I felt terrible about poor old Lenin,' Lottie continued unabashed. 'I took him for a thorough shampoo the next day to get rid of any taint.'

Hearing his name mentioned, and apparently none the worse for his encounter with the unwelcome passenger, Lenin woke from sleep beyond the bar and looked up expectantly.

'What did you do with the photograph, Trevor?' said Mr Disvan.

'Well, first off I thought to burn it—that's what I told Tania I'd done, but in fact I've got it here. Do you want to see it again?'

'Yes please.'

The picture was produced and for the second time we were able to see the little girl visible in the back of the car, with her arm cradled around the dog's neck and her snarling face close up against the window. As before, dark shadows covered most of her features.

'That's sure some trick of the light!' exclaimed Mr Wessner.

'Okay, okay,' said the landlord angrily wiping the bar top, 'so I was wrong. I freely admit it. There's no need to rub it in.'

'Yes, I think we can safely discount that theory, attractive as it was,' said Mr Disvan.

'So what is going on, then?' asked the landlord.

Trevor's retort was almost angry, and a look of frustration briefly occupied his features. 'If I knew that, I wouldn't be here asking you lot for advice, would I?'

'Now, now,' said Disvan, 'there's no call for harshness. We want to assist you. Just describe to us what happened to you today.'

'Okay, I will. Sorry I shouted, Barry.'

'Consider it forgotten,' said the landlord.

'Well anyway, nearly two months have passed since that incident with the dog as you know, and I'd almost succeeded in putting the matter aside. So all right, there's something peculiar in the back of my car. So all right, it makes me uneasy when I'm driving alone. But I can live with that. You simply pretend that it never happened and get on with life. After all, no one could force me to look at those two photographs, could they? We ought to be celebrating our exam results and various job offers instead of fretting about weird pictures, didn't we? Well, Tania was beginning to come round to that point of view and agreed to accept a lift into Guildford. Up to now she's been using the bus or train you see—anything rather than get in the car.'

'Well it's understandable, poor girl,' said Lottie.

'Yes, of course; I'm not blaming her. So there we were driving along with the radio on and everything seemed fine. Tania kept glancing over her shoulder but there was nothing there, and I didn't feel any more uncomfortable than usual in the car. There was a programme of 1960s' music on the radio, as I thought quite cheerful stuff really and, what with the sunshine and everything, we were in good spirits. That's when the news came on.'

'What of it?' said Mr Disvan.

'It said Russia had invaded Czechoslovakia.'

'First I've heard of it,' said Mr Patel. 'It wasn't on the six o'clock news.'

'And it went on to say that President Dubcek had been deposed.'

'But that was in 1968.'

'Precisely.'

'Oh dear.'

'We were listening to radio from the 1960s.'

'Are you sure?' said the landlord. 'Perhaps they were re-running a set of old programs.'

'I've rung the radio station and checked.'

'And is that all that happened?' asked Disvan.

'Hardly. The truth was just beginning to dawn on Tania and me when the radio program suddenly went off and something else came on.'

'What?'

'A scream. A long, high pitched, hate-filled scream.'

'A little girl's scream?'

'Precisely.'

'What did you do?'

'We ditched the car and got a taxi straight home. Doctor Bani-Sadr is round seeing Tania now and I've come out for a stiff drink. Gordon from the garage is going out to fetch the car back.'

'And what are you going to do now?' asked the landlady in a horrified tone.

Trevor's voice was full of determination and dark intent. 'Tomorrow, as soon as I wake, I'm going to take action.'

* * *

From his manner we had feared that the 'action' Trevor proposed would be both decisive and violent. Images of the offending car being found burnt out in a lay-by or at the bottom of a cliff suggested themselves. In the event, however, perhaps influenced by the moderating spirit of rational inquiry which had pervaded his university training, Trevor's action was to take the vehicle to be further tested.

'An old friend of mine in London has gone into photography,' he explained to us in the Argyll upon his return. 'He does stuff for advertising. Attractive pictures of meat balls and new brands of soup, that sort of thing, you know.'

We all nodded sagely, visualising such adverts while considering the frustration and futility of a life spent in this way.

'Well, he's got his own studio and we put the car in it and set up delayed action cameras all around. Then he took pictures from every conceivable angle over a period of twenty-four hours in all degrees of lighting and, I'm delighted to say, not a single one shows anything other than a normal car. If you want to see the proof, there's a hundred and fifty prints sitting in the back of the car for your inspection.'

No one seemed to want to take up this offer to examine the evidence for the vehicle's declared clean bill of health. It may have been that the need to enter the car in order to do so influenced our decision to decline.

'So where does that leave you?' said the landlord.

'Ah well, that's not all of my story. I wouldn't have been happy to leave it there. No, fortunately this chap up in London has a friend, a lecturer at the University College, who specialises in the technical aspects of photography. We went to see him with the original photographs and he reckons that he has the explanation for them.'

'A university lecturer you say?' asked Disvan.

'That's right. Apparently very prominent in his

field as well.'

'Now that's encouraging. What was his explanation?'

'It's the glass. Some freak effect in the make-up of the car windows bends and distorts light in some circumstances to give that image of the little girl. It's been documented before. He had a book with pictures that showed similar effects.'

'What, like the one we saw?' said the landlord.

'Well... almost. Most of them were more fuzzy than the first photographs we took, but it's recognisably the same phenomenon.'

'Right...' said Mr Patel. 'What did he have to say about the car radio incident, then?'

'Nothing. Like I said, he's an expert on photography, not electronics. That's my field.'

'So how would you explain the voice you told us about?'

'A freak effect, a drift of frequency that caught a snatch of another station, a burst of static that sounded a bit like a scream. Radios, especially wonky old car radios operating on the move, are quite capable of producing such a thing.'

'It seems like a lot of freak effects to afflict one car,' said Mr Disvan.

'Life's like that, Mr Disvan,' Trevor replied.

'I see.'

'I've never heard of such a thing,' said Mr Wessner.

Trevor seemed cheerfully confident about his explanation. 'Well such things do happen, Mr Wessner, whether they reach your ears or not.'

'Whippersnapper,' muttered Mr Wessner under his breath.

'So what have you done about all this, then?' asked Mr Disvan.

'I went straight from the lecturer's place to a

while-you-wait garage in Streatham and had every bit of glass in the car replaced.'

'Seems sensible,' said the landlord.

'Expensive, though,' added Mr Patel. 'If it were me... Well, I'd get a new car.'

'Tell me,' said Mr Disvan, 'does Tania travel in the car now?'

'No.'

'Ah.'

'Look, I know you lot don't believe what I'm saying,' the young man continued, 'so I'll have to prove it to you. Would you kindly oblige me with your new Polaroid please, Barry?'

'If you want,' replied the landlord. 'Mind you, it didn't show anything the first time, but when Lottie—'

'Yes I know, I know, but please just humour me.'

'Okay. Lottie! Camera please.'

A picture was duly taken and we awaited its development back in the bar.

'There you are,' said Trevor eventually, quite his old self again. 'Whip out the glass and wipe out the ghost—simple as that.'

'Don't think you're going to get Lenin in there again to prove your university man right' said Lottie defensively.

'There's no need. The story's over. Here you are, Barry, here's the two offending photos. You can pin them up on the holiday postcard board.'

The landlord looked at them gingerly but did not reach out to accept.

'No, thank you all the same. I'm not as convinced as you, if I must be honest. I wouldn't be happy having them in the Argyll. For my money, they show something not of this world and such things aren't meant to be on view.'

'Well said,' Lottie added.

'Oh ye of little faith!' Trevor said jokingly. 'Hasn't the twentieth century reached Binscombe yet?'

'We've still got it on approval,' growled the landlord, 'and haven't decided whether to keep it.'

* * *

Trevor Jones against the world—as later told to Mr Oakley

In honest truth, Trevor only felt around seventy-five percent of the confidence he had manifested to the clientele of the Argyll, but had felt obliged to put on a convincing show in front of the unenlightened. On emerging from the bar, his spirit of cheerful optimism returned as he saw the car, unoccupied and acquiescent, awaiting him. Having recourse to rational counsel from experts and professionals seemed to have purged the vehicle of the imaginary malign and brooding aura which had previously adhered to it. Consulting the joint wisdom of the villagers had had the opposite effect. Trevor now reproached himself for ever having placed reliance in their nth hand knowledge and handed down superstitions. How could he have been so unnerved as to panic in that way and surrender himself to beliefs straight out of the Dark Ages? They were decent folk in their way, but their time was gone.

Secretly, Trevor worried that there was a side to himself that would make willing obeisance to the irrational as they did. The danger of such a retrogressive slide was ever present. Even Mr Oakley, a well educated outsider, seemed increasingly that way inclined.

The engine started first time and Trevor pulled smartly away, consciously using his full driving skills to proceed as neatly and elegantly as possible. Made more than human by the addition of the machine's power and speed to his own, he felt his assurance in his own world view growing back to normal strength. Thus emboldened he turned on the car radio for the first time since the previous disturbing incident and, with the slightest twinge of relief, heard the (contemporary) sounds of Radio One come forth.

At that time of day there was only light traffic about, and Trevor decided not to go straight home but to see where road and whim would lead him for a short while. He felt as at peace as a man of his age and time ever would be and with this came a sense of gentle benevolence to his fellow man (men such as those who had 'reclaimed' his car for him). Consequently, contrary to his normal practice, he stopped to pick up a lone hitch-hiker even though he was a young man of somewhat shaggy appearance.

'Where are you heading?'

'Goldenford, please.'

'It's not far out of my way, I'll take you there. Hop in.'

'Thank you very much.'

The young man got in and they drove away.

'At the university are you?' asked Trevor.

'That's right.'

In the way of such things the two strictly temporary companions soon lapsed into silence. Only a few more minutes driving would bring them into town. The young student produced a packet of sweets from his combat jacket and popped one into his mouth.

'Want one?' he said.

'No thanks.'

'What about your daughter—would she like one?'

* * *

'Amen' said the Reverend Jagger.

'Amen' we answered raggedly.

'Well, that's about it,' continued the Rector of Saint Joseph's, Binscombe, 'though what good it will do I can't possibly say. I've never done an exorcism before, least of all on a car. It's a very unusual set of circumstances all round, really. I mean, I've heard of exorcisms on people sometimes, on houses occasionally, but on cars—never. The Bishop wasn't very happy about it, of course. However, in view of the evidence, he agreed we could go ahead providing it was discreetly done.'

'We're very grateful to you, Rector,' said Tania, 'Thank you for persuading him.'

'I'm not so sure it's me you should thank. The Bishop's final words to me were "if Disvan thinks it's necessary then go ahead", so perhaps you were more instrumental, Mr Disvan.'

'I think not, Rector. I've never met your Bishop.'

'No? Oh well, he seems to know of you.'

'Curious.'

'Yes.'

'Anyway,' said Tania, 'our thanks to whoever's responsible. Isn't that right, Trevor?'

He nodded in response.

'Are you not feeling any better?' enquired Mr Disvan solicitously.

'Yes I'm fine,' the young man replied, although everything from the slump of his shoulders to the shake in his fingertips served to deny this. Quite apart from the effects of the last incident, Trevor was now pressed, half willingly and half by dire necessity, into a world of demons and exorcisms where he was very far from home. The consequences of this clearly showed.

'Let's get inside,' said the Rector. 'There's quite a

nip in the air at this time in the morning.'

It was indeed only 6:00 a.m. when we, a small select number of invited people, had gathered in the rear car park of the Argyll (for reasons of convenience and concealment) to observe the service of exorcism. From opening address to closing dismissal, the operation took a mere ten minutes and the Reverend Jagger's final dispensing of holy water upon the car neatly coincided with the rising of the sun above the rooftops. It was getting perilously close to the time when the advance guard of the commuter army would be appearing, taking an illegal but long tolerated shortcut through the landlord's front car park on their madcap dash to their station. We had no wish to come under their incurious scrutiny in present circumstances, and so followed the Rector's advice to adjourn inside.

The landlord and Lottie, ever practical, had prepared some mulled beer to dispel the chill, physical and otherwise, and in due course the gathering became almost convivial.

The Reverend Jagger started on an ill-timed tale of an exorcism he had heard of while working with the RSPCK in Africa and the trail of horrible deaths it had left behind. Trevor looked at him with increasing horror and became even paler than hitherto. The hand holding his mug of beer drooped until the contents were close to spilling. Disvan, the landlord and I simultaneously noticed the effect that the story was having on the young man and saw the need to interrupt. Sadly, the landlord was the first to react.

'Are the police going to proceed with those dangerous driving charges, Trevor?'

Mr Disvan and I exchanged glances. It was not exactly the sort of intervention we could have hoped for, but at least the Rector's tale of possession and murder was halted.

Trevor took no notice, continuing to stare at and through the clergyman. Tania nudged him. 'Trevor, someone's talking to you.'

He came to suddenly. 'What?'

The landlord repeated his question.

'Ah... yes... apparently. My solicitor says that if I blame the hitch-hiker for distracting me I might get off with just a disqualification.'

'Have they located him yet?'

'No, he ran off into the woods by Saint Catherine's Mount and the University say that they haven't seen him since.'

'Poor boy,' said Lottie.

'To be honest,' said Mr Wessner, who had previously been in deep thought, 'I can't see why you don't resolve the whole matter by selling the damn car.'

'Or by destroying it,' agreed the Rector. 'Couldn't you put it through one of those crunching machines that turn motor cars into blocks of scrap?'

For a second, a weak spark of hope appeared in Trevor's eyes, but it quickly faded and died when Tania answered for him.

'No,' she said, 'that wouldn't resolve it—not at all. Either way we'd be passing the problem on to the new owner or the scrap dealer and it'd still leave it as a mystery. No, I've thought of doing what you suggest but it wouldn't be right.'

Lottie and Mr Disvan smiled at Tania in approval.

'In theory,' said the landlord, 'there shouldn't be a problem anymore, should there? Else what's the point of us getting up at this Godforsaken hour— begging your pardon, Padre—and having Mr Jagger here do his stuff?'

Trevor looked unconvinced but too lost to protest.

Mr Disvan now tried to repair the damage done.

'Would you care for me to drive you both home?'

'What, in our car?'

'Yes, I've no fear of it.'

'Would you?' she said.

'Certainly. The Reverend here has done what can be done to put it right and we should put some faith in his efforts.'

'Well, it would be nice at first to have some company, I must admit,' she said.

'If you wish, I'll come too,' said the Rector.

Trevor suddenly roused himself and reassumed, albeit by obvious force of will, his former robust manner.

'Thank you but no, that won't be necessary. It's very kind of you but I'm damned if I'm going to back down in the face of this nightmare. So okay, I've had to call in an exorcist; so all right, I'm out of my depth and in a strange world that doesn't make any sense to me. But I'm going to stay with this... thing—and see it through!'

The landlord applauded. 'Good for you, boy,' he said.

These words of Trevor's were more or less addressed to the company in general but now his tone suggested that he was talking to himself and vocalising some internal struggle. He spoke with genuine fervour. 'This is our world. We belong here. It has its own rules and laws and—it's more powerful than whatever's out there in that car!'

Doctor Bani-Sadr, a known rationalist who had nevertheless listened respectfully to the service of exorcism, joined in with the landlord's applause.

The Reverend Jagger and Mr Disvan exchanged apprehensive looks.

* * *

'Well?' said the landlord.

'No problems so far,' replied Trevor, 'It's as quiet as the... Well, nothing's happened, anyway.'

'The service must have worked,' Tania agreed.

'Have you told the Rector?' asked Mr Disvan.

'Yes,' said Tania, 'I rang him up. He sounded more relieved than us.'

'Well, that figures,' said Doctor Bani-Sadr, 'if you'll excuse me saying so. All that's at stake for you is a car, but for Jagger it's the reputation of his church and his whole system of beliefs that's on the line isn't it?'

'I don't think it is as simple as that, doctor,' said Mr Disvan. 'The rector didn't guarantee anything.'

'Don't know why you should stick up for him, Disvan, it's not as if you're one of his believers,' the doctor grumbled into his barley wine.

'That's neither here nor there.'

'I disagree...'

'The point is,' Tania interrupted firmly, 'that Reverend Jagger was kind enough to stretch a theological point in the first place in order to exorcise a car. I don't suppose it's done his career any great good in the Bishop's eyes. The further and crucial fact is that it appears to have worked.'

'So get shot of the car before something happens,' advised Mr Wessner.

'There may not be any need now,' said Trevor.

'Let's hope not,' said the landlord. 'Excuse me while I serve this customer.'

He moved off to attend to a little old lady who had just entered. I recognised her as the owner of one of the ancient terraced houses directly opposite the pub. It was a rare event for either her or her diminutive husband to actually ever enter the Argyll.

'What can I get for you, Mrs Singer?' he asked.

'Nothing. I didn't come over here to buy anything. I came over to complain.'

'What about, dear? People been knocking your hedge around again at closing time, have they?'

'Yes, but that's not what I'm complaining about. I want to know who owns the yellow Fiesta parked out front.'

The public bar instantly fell silent.

'I do,' said Trevor with commendable calm.

'Well, young man, you ought to be ashamed of yourself. And you, young lady. Your little girl's been screaming and crying her eyes out for the best part of an hour. Isn't it time you did something about it?'

A wild light blazed in Trevor's eyes.

'You're absolutely right,' he said, 'it's high time I did something about it!'

Thus saying he dashed from the pub.

* * *

'Where do you think he was heading, Stan?' said Mr Disvan.

A group of half a dozen of us were gathered round the Community Policeman's bed in Saint Dismas's Hospital in Goldenford.

'From what you've said, my guess is that he was going to Pavlik Kolakowski's scrap yard between Goldenford and the Winchester roundabout. He's got a vehicle crusher there. Judging by where the car ended up, I should imagine that was his intention. Of course we'll never know for sure.'

'How did you come to get involved, then?' asked Mr Patel.

A senior looking nurse who had been hovering around us, pretending to be occupied in some task, intervened at this point.

'Please, gentlemen,' she said, 'remember that the constable is still technically in a state of shock. Don't overtax him with questions or make him relive whatever upset him.'

'Ignore her,' the policeman said, 'she just wants to keep me helpless and in her power for as long as possible. But for her say-so I could have gone home this morning. I'm all right, I tell you.'

'The doctor and I think otherwise. Would you like a cup of tea?'

'If it'll get rid of you, yes please. Anyway, gentlemen, to continue...'

'Are you up to it?' Mr Disvan interposed.

'Insofar as I'll ever be, yes.'

'Okay then, carry on.'

'Right. The answer to your question Sammy, before we were so rudely interrupted, is that I got called out to investigate reports of an abandoned car, partially obstructing the flow of traffic, on the very edge of my patch. I thought nothing of it because it's surprising how many of them you get, quite serviceable cars many of them, until I recognised it as the one young Trevor Jones has been riding around in. What I didn't know about was all the trouble he and Tania had been having—why wasn't I told?'

'It wasn't really a "polis" matter, Stan,' said Mr Disvan, 'and you just didn't happen to be around at the right time when things were going on.'

The recumbent policeman sighed.

'Oh well, anyway, there the car was, abandoned on the inside lane looking as if it had skewed to a halt diagonally across the road. No sign of Trevor about, no note left or anything. A bit of a puzzle, I thought. So I looked inside and noticed that the keys were still in the ignition.'

'But the engine was off?' I asked.

'Yes, the motor was quite cold. Well, as the station had rightly said, the car was obstructing traffic and so I got in with the intention of driving it over into a lay-by and out of harm's way until Trevor could be located. Then, as I turned the keys, the radio suddenly came on—it must have been left running, you see. As God is my witness, you must believe me, Trevor's voice came out of the radio together with that of a little girl talking to him and tormenting him. Trevor was screaming and begging for her to stop.

I listened for a little while, and then the next thing I knew was waking up in here. Very embarrassing for a policeman of all people to faint like that.'

Nobody responded for a minute or so and then Mr Disvan quietly spoke for us all.

'What exactly was she saying to Trevor, Stan?'

What little colour there was in the policeman's face rapidly fled. He seemed to forget our presence.

'Stan?' Disvan prompted.

He looked at us again but this time as if at strangers.

'Believe me, you really don't want to know. Nurse! Can you get these visitors to go, please?'

*　*　*

'Well, thank you for telling me what you can,' said Tania. 'Would you like another cup of tea, Mr Disvan?'

'No thank you.'

'You're taking it very well, Miss Knott,' said Doctor Bani-Sadr, 'but a reaction may set in. I'll prescribe you something to help you sleep.'

'That's thoughtful. I feel okay at the moment, but I'm not so sure about when I'm left on my own.'

'Why not go and stay at your parents?' I asked in as kindly a voice as possible.

'No, I prefer to stay here in case he returns.'

'That's far from likely, I'm afraid,' said Mr Disvan.

'Possibly so, but it could happen. Trevor's not dead you know.'

'No... but at the risk of seeming cruel, my dear, the day must come, sooner or later, when you'll have to act as if he is.'

With anyone else I would have described her reply as vehement, but with Miss Knott that would have been too harsh a term.

'That day will never come, Mr Disvan. Trevor is alive and with us even though we can't speak to him.'

'To be precise,' said the landlord, 'he's parked in your garage.'

Mr Disvan reproved him with a look.

'Sorry,' he said, 'I didn't mean it to sound quite that blunt. It just came out that way. What will you do with yourself now?'

"What can I do? If I was to sell the car I'd lose track of Trevor—and lay someone else open to the risk of sharing his fate. If I had it destroyed... well, that'd be like killing him.'

'I doubt the car would allow itself to be destroyed' said Mr Disvan. 'That was Trevor's fatal—if you'll excuse the term, Tania—mistake. He acted rashly and the car's owner, the real owner, defended itself.'

'Probably you're right, although I'll never see it that way. I hate the car's owner.'

'Of course you do, that's more than understandable.'

'So the car will just have to stay there in the garage. I'll look after it, make sure it lives as long as I live and, who knows, perhaps I'll wake up one day to find that Trevor's found his way out. It's not the marriage I would have dreamed of, but it's better than nothing.'

Quiet fell upon the room as each of us in our own

way pondered the implications of Tania's words. Disvan looked at her with something approaching admiration and even I, not an unduly sentimental man, was touched by her steadfast loyalty—however misguided.

The silence, being maintained, became uncomfortable and Tania appeared to be slipping into a dark reverie as she contemplated the lonely life of vigilance before her. We racked our brains for some words of consolation that would not be entirely facile. Alas, as before, the landlord's mind was more agile and less discriminating than ours and he spoke first.

'Well, at least you can still go out for a drive together,' he said.

Tania looked at him for a moment and then began to weep as if only death would stop her.

Waiting for a Bus

'Have you met Bob Springer, Mr Oakley?'

'I don't believe I have, Mr Disvan. How do you do, Mr Springer?'

'Not so bad, thank you. And please call me Bob like everyone else does. How long have you been living in our village, Mr Oakley?'

'Three or four years in all, though my family originally came from here. Isn't that so, Mr Disvan?'

Disvan obviously thought a sage nod was all the response required by my semi-rhetorical question, but I noticed that Springer watched keenly for his answer before continuing the conversation.

'Not long then.'

'No.'

'I see.'

A silence fell on our little gathering as we all regrouped in search of something else to say and the pause, although slightly awkward, gave me an opportunity to study this new acquaintance and to judge whether the effort was merited.

Bob Springer was, I decided, a perfectly ordinary and unexceptional little old man; one of the seemingly inexhaustible supply of such who quietly inhabited the obscurer corners of Binscombe's pubs and parks for a few years before drifting off unnoticed into the greater quiet of the grave. I'd also observed that a female of the species existed although their natural habitat was the local Anglican church. However, that's another tale.

Then, as I looked closer, I realised that I was wrong in my initial evaluation of him and that his ordinariness was so extreme as to be far from ordinary; that he was unexceptional to a thoroughly exceptional degree. This peculiarity could perhaps account for the fact that, despite having lived a number of years in this smallish community, I did not recall having seen Mr Springer even once before, although I was now quite willing to believe that our paths could have crossed many times each and every day. If they had, it was not surprising that he'd escaped my attention so far for he was a singularly unnoticeable sort of man. Unbidden, the whimsical thought occurred to me that he would have made the perfect assassin.

'Would you like a drink, gentlemen?' he said.

'Well... I don't know,' I replied. 'I was just thinking I ought to be getting home.'

Springer looked at me with an expression of grim, almost threatening, intent that took me by surprise and said 'I insist' in a tone that, insofar as he could manage, brooked no refusal.

I could think of no pressing reason why I should give offence, however inexplicable, by refusing his request cum command.

'Very well, that's kind of you. I'll have a pint of Directors please.'

'And you, Disvan?'

'If you do insist, I'll have my usual, thank you.'

Springer, now suddenly a meek and mild little old man once again, took our glasses and scuttled up to the bar.

'What got into him?' I said to Mr Disvan who seemed as unruffled as ever by the strange behaviour of others.

'He wants someone to walk him home I expect.

That's the danger of talking to Bob Springer near to closing time.'

'Why? What's the matter? Is someone waiting outside for him?'

'As ever, Mr Oakley, you have the strange knack of hitting the nail right on the head completely by accident. Leastways, I assume it's by accident. Maybe your ancient Binscombe blood shows through in the form of second sightedness.'

'I'll assume that you jest, Mr Disvan although, being the master of enigma that you are, it's never easy to tell.'

'Sticks and stones, Mr Oakley, mere sticks and stones.'

'Careful now, he's coming back.'

'Here we are, gents, drinks all round.'

'Many thanks, Mr Springer—or Bob, should I say.'

'Not at all, your very good health.'

I noticed that Mr Disvan did not straight away take a drink in response to this toast as we did, but sat quite still giving Springer a very cool look indeed. The old man pretended not to notice that he was under this scrutiny even though it was pretty open. Instead he gave himself body and soul to an observation of the table top. At length Disvan broke the silence.

'Talking of good health, I suppose these drinks mean you want us to escort you home.'

Springer's expression was a blend of relief and embarrassment but his reply was both speedy and decisive:

'Yes please.'

Disvan turned to me: 'Do you have the time to spare to walk Bob home, Mr Oakley?'

'I suppose so, if it's necessary.'

'I'd be very grateful if you would,' said Springer eagerly. 'It'd save so much time.'

'Why?'

'Because if you two come along I won't have to walk the long way home all through Compton.'

'Where do you live then?'

'Trebizond Crescent.'

'But Compton's miles out of your way if you're going to Trebizond Crescent.'

'Exactly.'

'Mr Disvan, can you shed any light on this please?'

'Surely anything I say will be construed to be enigmatic.'

'Quite possibly, but even so...'

At this point our joint host interrupted my visibly flailing questions and brought debate to a close by interposing the call, 'Time gentlemen please!'

'Will you do this for me?' said Springer plaintively.

'Well, okay, if that's what you want. Are you game, Mr Disvan?'

'Yes.'

Mr Springer beamed with pleasure or some such feeling. 'That's marvellous, I'll be home in time to watch the snooker.'

'Well I won't now' said Disvan.

'You could watch it at my place I suppose, but you know the wife's a tartar about visitors.'

'Indeed I do, Bob.'

'That's unworthy of you, Mr Disvan. My problem shouldn't deprive me of the right to some dignity and courtesy, you know.'

'Quite right, well said. I apologise.'

'Thank you.'

'Look, can we go now?' I interposed. 'I have to be up early to go to work tomorrow.'

'Certainly, certainly,' said Springer in a placatory way, 'the sooner the better.'

We left along with the rest of the pub's patrons but

soon lost them in the maze of darkened streets as each went their separate way. There was no conversation in our little group and I did not press any further for an explanation from Springer or Disvan. If indeed there was an explanation for this present episode (and one could not count on it in present company) then its revelation must await some future time, for I was in no mood for long stories or excuses.

Trebizond Crescent, our destination, was not a long way from The Duke of Argyll but it seemed far enough that night when there appeared to be no good reason to make the trip. Consequently I began to harbour a degree of mild resentment towards the man who had set me upon it and answered somewhat sharply when, halfway along, he made a further demand.

'Eyes left!' Springer hissed.

'What?'

'Eyes left, you fool!'

'Who the hell do you think you're talking to?'

'Humour him, Mr Oakley,' said Disvan in a neutral tone, 'he thinks he's doing you a favour.'

'Eyes left! Don't look over there or he'll see you.'

'Who will?'

'It doesn't matter, just don't look and keep walking.'

Springer seemed genuinely alarmed, indeed almost frantic, and was, I observed, marching ahead very briskly with his face turned firmly to the left. Disvan, presumably by way of compromise, was staring at the ground as he walked along.

As previously explained, I was in a recalcitrant frame of mind and little disposed to stand any more nonsense from the old man. I therefore stopped and looked in the direction forbidden me but saw nothing unusual. Exactly as on our side of the road a strip of wooded wasteland bordered the pavement and beyond that the lights of a few large houses, well set back from the road, could be seen. Directly opposite me was a bus shelter of the more modern type lit by its own neon filament, but no-one was standing by it or sitting on its obviously older bench seat. Apart from ourselves the whole road was deserted and empty even of motor traffic and I could see no-one or no-thing whose gaze I should avoid as Springer insisted.

In the time it took to satisfy myself of this my two companions had progressed a further hundred yards up the road where they now waited for me. I hastened to join them.

'There's absolutely no-one over there, Springer. What on earth were you on about?'

'That was a very silly thing you did, Mr Oakley, if I may say so.'

'Why?'

'You may have been lucky enough not to see him but he was studying you—rest assured.'

'Who, for God's sake?'

'No blasphemy please, Mr Oakley,' said Disvan quietly.

'I'm sorry but really... this is ridiculous. Just look for yourself, Mr Springer, back down the road. There's not a soul about.'

'I daren't,' Springer said, and kept his attention fixed firmly to the front.

'Well, if you won't, you won't, I suppose.'

'No I won't. Let's move on, please.'

And this we did without further debate, albeit with bad grace on my part.

Ten more minutes of silent and brisk walking brought us at last to Springer's house. Once there he made for the door like a drowning man, pausing only to shout a seemingly genuine 'thank you very much' at us before slamming it shut. We then heard the rattling of chains and sliding of bolts as fortress Springer was made secure for the night.

'What the bloody hell was that all about, Mr Disvan?'

'That, Mr Oakley, was all about a man's complete submission to fear.'

'Very enigmatic.'

'But true nevertheless.'

'Tell me no more. In less than seven hours I have to be up and about again yet I'm needlessly still out in the cold, twenty minutes walk from my house. In fact that thought makes me feel more fractious than I already am and therefore I've run out of curiosity for today.'

'I quite understand. After knowing Bob Springer for all these years and despite understanding his problem, even I find it hard it to be patient with him.'

I fully recognised this to be a fine example of what I called Mr Disvan's 'hook lines', whereby each answer he provided carried not merely the seed but the ripe, ready to drop, fruit of another question. It was a great temptation, despite my professed lack of curiosity, to ask just what Springer's apparently readily understandable problem was, but by an act of will I managed to break the question-and-answer chain.

'Doubtless the explanation that I feel entitled to will wait a day or two more after 'all these years', Mr Disvan. Goodnight to you.'

'As you say, it can wait—forever if need be—and anyway it's best that he tell you himself why he's so afeared and why you've been put out. Goodnight then.'

The shortest paths to our respective homes lay in different directions and so I strode off Binscombe-ward alone. This waste of time, this loss of supper, snooker and sleep I'd already put down to mere local folly of which there was no shortage. But even so, as I walked, I found that of their own volition, my eyes searched intently the dark shadows of that side of the road forbidden by Mr Springer.

* * *

'Look out, he's here again!'

'Avoid his eye and keep talking.'

'Too late—he's seen me.'

'It's another late night for us then.'

'Don't bet on it.'

'Here he is.'

'Mr Disvan and Mr Oakley, how are you?'

'Very well thank you, Bob.'

'Would you like a drink, gentlemen?'

'Not if it obliges us to chaperon you home again, thank you all the same.'

My pre-conceived, perhaps somewhat harsh response earned me one of Disvan's rare full-face stares. His expression was, as ever, inscrutable and the meaning of these admonitions or questions or whatever they were had to be guessed from the context of the occasion. In present circumstances I took it to signify some surprise on his part at my uncharacteristic lack of charity.

I'd observed before the surprising power of these visual shots across-the-bow upon the locals but was even more surprised to find an urgent desire to appease evoked in myself by the same means. Did this imply that I, a foreigner in their terms, and an 'educated' man to boot, was becoming subject to the tribal mores of Binscombe?

'I'm sorry, that wasn't really called for. It's just that... well, I don't want to be late home tonight.'

'That's all right, I understand,' he said in a voice that was indeed full of sad understanding. 'Mind if I join you?'

'No, please do.'

He sat down and toyed absently with one of the empty beer bottles on the table.

'Of course,' he then said abruptly, 'Mr Disvan says I'm a fool to live in such fear but then again, with all respect, he's not had to suffer what I've suffered.'

'I think that that's irrelevant,' said Disvan.

'Many things in this world are irrelevant or illogical but are still powerful forces nevertheless.'

An attempt at profundity was the last thing I was expecting from a man of such surpassing anonymity, and I felt a spark of revived interest in what he was obviously bursting to tell.

'That's very true,' I said.

Springer perhaps mistook interest for sympathy and turned to me as if to an ally.

'Mr Disvan says that, having been caught once, I'm in no further danger, but that's easy for him to say and besides, how can he be sure?'

'Now, now, Bob,' said the man in question, 'you know me better than that. I don't say things for effect and I wouldn't state things of which I'm not sure.'

'No doubt what you say is true, Mr Disvan, but I can't help my fear.'

Successfully hooked at last I could not forbear to indulge my curiosity. 'Fear of whom?'

Springer looked at Disvan in a querying manner and he, by way of reply, merely shrugged. This seemed to answer whatever doubt held him back and the old man could then unload his burden.

'Fear of the person or thing that took forty years of my life.'

'Who was that?'

'I don't know.'

'You mean someone took forty years of your life but you don't know their name?'

'No, he never told me it—not in all that time. His name's not all that important.'

'No?'

'No, not really.'

'Well, how were all those years stolen from you, then?'

'By holding me captive so that the active years of my life passed me by and were wasted in nothingness.'

'That's very serious. Who was responsible, then? The state?'

'Certainly not, I've never ever been in trouble with the law.'

'Some person, then...'

'In a manner of speaking.'

I sighed, being somewhat exasperated, and tried another approach. 'Well, where were you held prisoner then?'

'At the bus stop.'

My initial response was one of anger at being so obviously taken for a fool but this was soon overridden by the transparent sincerity of the old man's face. Nevertheless my response was still rich with sarcasm. 'You were imprisoned for forty years at a bus stop, were you?'

'Not any bus stop; the bus stop on the way to my house. But essentially, yes, that's correct.'

'If that's so, I ask once again: who by?'

'By the creature that waits there.'

'And that's the reason you won't pass by it on your own?'

'Exactly. He might see me and make me wait with him again.'

'But if you're with other people that can't happen?'

'I'm not sure but it seems a lot less likely.'

'Explain this to me.'

'What's to tell? I've told you it all.'

'It's not much of a tale for an event of forty years duration.'

'Time itself means very little. What is there to say of an accountant's life even if he lives to be a hundred? Nothing very much happened to me in those forty years so there's nothing much to recount.'

'Go on, Bob,' said Disvan, 'you ought to tell him the full story.'

Springer took this in and then turned to address me. 'Do you want that? Do you genuinely want to understand why I am as I am?'

'Yes,' I replied in all truthfulness. 'Tell me how you were deprived of the days of your youth.'

'My youth?' He chewed upon that bitter notion before continuing. 'Yes, that's what I lost, I suppose. And my young manhood and early middle age as well. I was only in my twenties when I was captured, you see.'

'How did it occur?'

'On a ordinary day, or evening to be more precise. I was going to get a bus into Goldenford to see a movie; on my own as usual. It was about sevenish. I was done up to the nines and I can remember very clearly that the sun was almost down and it was drizzling. The shelter wasn't there in those days, just the stop and the bench set back from the road, and I recall getting quite wet and feeling miserable.

'Then, just a few moments before the bus would arrive—for you could trust the timetables then—I heard a voice call me by name. That surprised me because I'd thought I was alone but when I turned round I could see that there was an old man sitting on the seat and he was beckoning me. There didn't seem to be anything really amiss although I felt sure there'd been no-one on the seat when I'd arrived. Even so I put that out of my mind for I very often travelled from that stop and consequently felt pretty much at ease there.

' "How can I help you?" I said, going up close to the person who'd spoken to me. It was nearly dark by that time, you see, and all I could make out was the outline of the old boy.

' "You can wait with me," he said back.

'Well, I didn't like his tone at all. It sounded very bitter, vicious almost, but I was an obliging sort of young man, very reluctant to give offence (more fool me) and so I said, "Very well," and sat down beside him.

' "Do I know you?" I enquired, for he'd approached me by name.

' "No," he said, "but I know you."

' "How so?"

' "Because I've often seen you here."

'Well, he sounded so nasty and unfriendly that I let it go at that and we waited on in silence.'

'Till when?'

'Till the bus arrived, Mr Oakley. Then by the light the bus gave out I saw that it was no man I was sitting alongside, leastways it may have been a man once but no longer. Horrible it was, pink and shrivelled and hairless and the skin on its face was taut and shiny. I could see its bared teeth and empty eye-sockets and it said:

' "You can wait with me."

'As you might imagine, I screamed and went to make a run for it but found I couldn't. No noise came from my lips and I remained rooted to my seat next to that... thing.'

'What about the bus?'

'That was almost the worst bit. The buses always stopped you see, just to check there was no-one waiting on the bench which was usually in shadow. I stared straight at the driver and, as I thought, he looked straight back at me. I even, in my distress, waved my arms at him but then he just turned his head and drove off. I realised then that, the Lord have mercy on me, I was no longer visible to the world of men.

'I watched, with a yearning I can't convey to you, the lights of the bus go off into the distance and the thing beside me chuckled—the sort of laugh cruel children make. And that's when it all began.'

'For forty solid years?'

'Almost, but not quite, to the day. Buses came and went—with decreasing frequency as the years went by I might add. Queues formed and then boarded, day succeeded day and season succeeded season, but still I was held there.'

'But what about food and drink, what about winter weather, cramp and things of that nature?'

'I never seemed to be hungry or thirsty, the cold and wind passed around me and whatever happened in the real world appeared not to be applicable to me. All I was allowed to do was wait. Wait with that foul creature.'

'That's appalling!'

'You can't imagine how appalling. Please don't get the impression that I didn't try to save myself because for the first few weeks I did little else. Every bus that arrived I begged and pleaded to be allowed to board it and every queue that formed I shouted and waved at but, all in all, I might just as well as saved my breath. People I'd grown up with waited just a few feet away, some even sat on the seat with us, but none of them could see or hear me.

'Once my dear mother, God rest her soul, came there and waited for a bus and I nearly went berserk trying to catch her attention. She seemed to realise something was wrong for she got fidgety and uneasy and kept looking round for whatever it was that was disturbing her, but when she did she looked straight through me.

'Eventually her bus came and she got on and once she was sitting down she stared at the bench as if she knew her son was sitting there and she continued to look as the bus drew away.

'That was very bitter. I never saw her again, for I later found out that she died soon after.

'How that creature laughed to see my tears that day and his every laugh sounded like the death of a baby on Christmas Eve. In my fury and horror I struck him but his flesh burned like acid and where I'd touched him my skin smoked. Look, the scars still show.'

It was true. A wide band of skin across each of his knuckles was brownish, twisted and quite dead.

'After that experience it was hard to imagine anything worse happening and so, after a fashion, I resigned myself to my fate. Still I asked to board each bus that came but the creature would just snap 'No!' in its nasty voice and that was that.

'With the passing of the years I grew to be almost philosophical about my predicament and took pleasure in watching the leaves on the trees change colour and all the other slow annual mutations in the rest of nature, for that was something I'd never had the time for up to then. Bit by bit I observed different buses come into service, all efficient and new, and then see them pass through their working lives till their engines were crotchety and their livery battle-worn. Watching the changes in people's fashions was interesting too, spring clothes, winter clothes and then back to spring again and new styles kept appearing as well. Quite fascinating really, if you've got nothing else to do.

'There were also moments of relative excitement like when workmen came to erect a shelter and light in... 1973 I think, and when an advertising station was put up about a year later. After that I had the pleasure of watching the advertisement posters being changed at regular intervals and it allowed me to keep in touch with things in some small way.

'I noticed that I was getting older but, since otherwise time was suspended for me, I learnt just to relax and observe, which is something few other people have the opportunity to do in this world. In time, you see, all Binscombe life passed by my bus stop.'

'You make it sound almost idyllic!'

'No, it wasn't that for I was held against my will, remember, and that fact coloured everything else. And, if the creature even suspected that I was taking pleasure in something, it would talk to me.'

'What about?'

'It is best, believe me, for your sake that you don't know. Suffice to say that he said bitter and twisted things, of individuals queuing for a bus, for instance, that showed people in a low and degraded light or emphasised the misery and futility of human life as he saw it. His words were designed to produce an effect in me. Whether they also represented the truth or not I've no idea.'

'How did it end?'

'As simply as it began. One day a bus arrived as per normal and the creature said, "Here is your bus." Suddenly I found that I could move and I saw that the driver's eyes were focused on me. He could actually see me! Despite forty years disuse my legs could still carry me as if I'd merely had a short sit-down and, as you might expect, I was on that bus like a streak of lightning. Then, just as the doors closed behind me, I heard the creature say, 'Thank you for waiting with me.' The doors slid shut, and when I turned round to look I couldn't see the thing, even though the last words it'd said were still ringing in my ears. Then the bus pulled away.

That wasn't the end of all my problems by any means. In effect, one major affliction was replaced with myriad minor ones. You can't just leave your life for forty years and expect to take up the reins again on your return. Difficulties began from the moment I boarded that long delayed bus. Take for instance the problem with paying my fare. I'd missed out on decimal currency, you see. I knew nothing about it and the driver wouldn't accept the coins I offered him. He thought I was either drunk or a joker when I handed him three old pennies. When he told me how much the fare really was, it was my turn to think that it was he who was joking—inflation being another thing I'd yet to learn about.

'Anyway, to cut a long story short, my mother's house had been sold many years before. I'd paid no National Insurance so there was no pension awaiting me. Most of my old friends were dead or gone away, and all in all I had to start from scratch.

'In time, of course, everything came together. I found a place to live, I caught up on forty years of world history in the public library, I even got married and God knows (begging your pardon Disvan) she's been a solace, bless 'er. So here I am. My life's not so bad, but I've got a lot of catching up to do and that's why I've no intention of ever being made to wait for a bus again.'

'Do you think then that the creature is still there?'

'I don't know. I just assume it is and act accordingly. You see, I've been free for a number of years now and for all I know the thing may be getting lonely and in need of company again, so I'm not inclined to put the matter to the test.'

'I get it. So that's why you won't pass the bus stop on your own.'

'Exactly.' He paused, something clearly bothering him, and then continued in a rush of words. 'Tell me, Mr Oakley, do you believe that what I've told you is true?'

I considered the possibility of this while studying Springer's guileless, indeed vacant, face and found that an honest answer came to me easily.

'I've only lived here a short time, but long enough not to totally discount what you say.'

'That is a good answer—if slightly enigmatic,' said Disvan.

'Mr Disvan believes me, don't you?'

'I do, Bob. I accept what you tell us. But what I don't accept, as I've said to you many times before, is that you're in any further danger. You've done your stint of waiting and your company is no longer required.'

'Fine words, but I'll not believe them till I'm safely in my grave.'

'As you wish.'

I felt some need to make amends for my earlier incivility and in debt to Springer for his candidness.

'In that case,' I said, 'I—or perhaps we...' Disvan nodded in affirmation, 'would be happy on this occasion to provide an escort to your house.'

The old man thanked us gravely. 'I'll not impose on your good nature with any regularity but tonight I would welcome a short walk home and human company on the way. I'm obliged to you.'

* * *

And, at closing time, an escort and human company we duly provided. As we passed the bus shelter of which we had spoken all evening Springer once again asked that we avert our eyes and quicken the pace, and this time I did so with good grace although not before noticing that the stop was devoid of any life I could see.

Once we were past this lonely spot we slowed to a normal walk again and I felt able to ask the one question—the one question, at least, that seemed capable of any resolution—that still puzzled me.

'Bob, why do you think you were chosen?'

'In what way?'

'I mean chosen out of all the people who ever waited at that stop. Why did the creature select you in particular to keep it company?'

'I honestly don't know. It was just written, I suppose.'

'I think that's true,' interposed Disvan, 'but not to the extent that it was just a random act of fate. I think, if you'll please excuse me saying so, Bob, that you never were a man marked out for great deeds or an eventful life. It was written very plainly on your face even when I knew you as a boy.'

'That may be so.'

'And being such a very unexceptional, ordinary man made you ideal material if someone was to be snatched from life for forty years. It may be that the powers that rule us would only sanction such an event if the disruption to the normal world was minimal, as it was in your case.'

'True—cruel, mind you—but quite possibly true. I had no career worth speaking of, few friends to miss me, and mother was all the family I'd got.'

'There you are, then.'

Disvan's last comment could either be taken as rounding off the successful presentation of his case or as the announcement of Springer's safe arrival home, for we were indeed before his door.

Lost in private thoughts the old man let himself in and almost forgot, in his preoccupation, to bid us farewell. Just as the door was about to shut, he came to and said, 'Thank you gentlemen for your patience. Goodnight.'

'Goodnight,' we replied in kind and immediately set off home as if eager to be free of his company—although I, at least, was not.

'I'll make a minor detour and walk with you part of the way,' said Mr Disvan.

'That would be welcome,' I said and we walked along in silence until once again we drew close to the yellow-lit, deserted bus shelter. As though by prior consent we halted opposite it, looking perhaps for tokens to confirm Springer's story. In its present condition the shelter looked the very epitome of lifeless anticipation.

At length I finally broke the silence. 'Do you believe him?'

'Well, he certainly did disappear for forty years.'

'But do you believe him?'

'Yes I do.'

'And would you wait for a bus at that stop?'

'I rarely would have occasion to, but the straight answer is no, I wouldn't.'

'Then how can you be so sure that Mr Springer isn't in danger?'

Disvan paused, exhaling air and sadness through his teeth.

'Partly because he's done his turn but mainly because soon after he arrived back in Binscombe, ten years ago now, young Mark Brown went missing. He often travelled by bus, you see, and he was most certainly a very unremarkable chap.

'No, Mr Oakley, I don't think there's anything for us to fear over there at the moment because, as the saying goes, two's company—but three's a crowd.'

All Roads Lead to Rome

The sight of a stranger in the Duke of Argyll was always of interest, because of its mild rarity value, and to see an unaccompanied young lady was doubly so. Accordingly, I was both surprised and intrigued, on approaching the premises one summer's evening, to spy Mr Disvan sitting in the pub garden deep in conversation with an attractive woman whose face was unknown to me. I hesitated to intrude upon them and so continued on into the bar.

'You're late,' said the landlord in a mock chiding voice.

'Possibly,' I replied, 'it being our busy time of year, I had to work on beyond normal hours.'

'I see,' said the landlord who never bothered to hide his lack of interest or indeed belief in anything that happened beyond the boundaries of Binscombe.

I decided to turn the conversation so as to satisfy my curiosity and to engage the landlord's attention all in one.

'Who's Mr Disvan talking to out in the pub garden?'

'I'm not sure, but I think she's one of the Diggers.'

'Diggers?'

'He means the archaeologists,' said Doctor Bani-Sadr. 'They're excavating up on top of Binscombe ridge, near Mellersh Farm.'

'There was something about it in the *Advertiser*,' said the landlord.

'Ah, is that it. For a while I thought it might be his long lost daughter or even a girlfriend!'

My comment, intended to be humorous, fell horribly flat. Nobody laughed or smiled or had anything to say at all. They all looked away and acted for a moment as if I was not there. Having obviously breached local etiquette, I thought it best to temporarily remove myself from the scene.

'Do you think they would mind if I joined them?'

'Course not,' said the landlord, 'there's nothing going on between them, is there?'

'No. Well, I think I'll take my drink outside and see you all later.'

'Suit yourself.'

I left the bar with the unpleasant sensation, whether true or false I could not say, of having several sets of eyes trained upon my retreating back. The silence was maintained until I had passed through the door and then I heard the low hum of conversation start up again.

I shrugged off the feeling of unease that the incident had produced in me. Such solecisms were fairly frequent and hard to avoid in Binscombe's complex tribal set-up, even for people such as I, who had lived there for years. Their occurrence just had to be accepted and, since forgiveness was always swift, time spent worrying about them was time wasted.

I walked across the rear car park where, some time ago now, Trevor Jones's car had been exorcised, and passed through the wicker gate into the Beer Garden. Although it was a warm evening without a hint of a breeze, Mr Disvan and his companion were the only people out enjoying their drinks in the dying sunshine, and all the other tables still had their chairs stacked upon them. My approach was eventually noticed and the two turned to study the newcomer. Mr Disvan, of course, instantly recognised me but the woman took no notice of this and continued to appraise me with a very cool, self-assured gaze. I recognised the technique from long sad years of London social warfare and so returned her look with equal candour. She was in her early thirties (or possibly late twenties with premature wear) and, although no attempt was made to emphasise the fact, she was, as I had earlier spotted, definitely attractive in a challenging sort of way. She wore a bib and braces outfit with a cheerful red scarf wound into her hair, and a pint of dark beer stood before her on the garden table.

'Ah, Mr Oakley,' said Disvan, 'glad to see you. Bit late, aren't you?'

'I had to work.'

'Busy time of year in your business, I expect.'

'That's right, it is actually. How did you know?'

'Commonsense.'

'I see. Anyway, leaving that all aside, I wonder if you'd mind if I joined you? I've said the wrong thing again in there.'

'Mind? No, I insist.'

'Thank you.'

'Mr Oakley, I'd like you to meet Elaine, she's one of the archaeologists working up on the ridge.'

'I'm pleased to meet you, Elaine. How's the work developing?'

'Handsomely, thank you—and please call me Ellie, I much prefer it.'

'Okay.'

'What's wrong with Elaine?' asked Mr Disvan curiously.

'I don't know. I'm just not at ease with it so I use an alternative.'

'How strange. There's no bad connotations to it that I'm aware of. It's an old French version of the Greek name Helen—very ancient as you know.

There's also Arthurian links to it via Tennyson and Mallory—"Elaine, the lily maid of Astolat" who had "that love which was her doom"'. A lovely old story.'

'Very nice, I'm sure, but I still prefer Ellie.'

'Ellie thinks,' said Mr Disvan, 'that they've uncovered, if you'll excuse the pun, good evidence for continuity of use between the Iron Age and Romano-British cemeteries up there.'

'Really? What about the barrow, though?'

'Ah, well that's the most interesting part of all, isn't it, Ellie?

The lady in question was looking at us with open approval.

'You know, you people round here are really amazing. I've been digging all over, and everywhere else I've been all the locals want to know is if we've found any gold or skeletons—skeletons or gold every time. Here, though, people ask me about evidence for continuity of settlement, about cemetery lay-out and burial practises—all the sort of stuff only us professionals are supposed to be interested in. What is it about Binscombe people?'

'We're very keen on knowing about our past here, Ellie.'

'And if we're not to start with, then Mr Disvan makes sure that we are sooner or later. It was him who told me about the cemeteries up on the ridge—I wouldn't have known about them otherwise. With the best will in the world, there's just not the time to read up old archaeological reports and such like, so we rely on Mr Disvan here to be our fountain of knowledge.'

'Even so, it's pretty unusual to find an archaeologically educated public—and very gratifying.'

'Why should you care?' I said.

'Else what's the point of what we're all doing? Why

go on excavating and producing reports if the society they're intended for doesn't give a damn?'

'You could say the same about anything that's not strictly practical.'

Ellie reached for her packet of cigarettes and lit one.

'Yeah, that's true. I'm overstating the case. Anyway, I'd still be an archaeologist even if I was the only one in the world who was the least bit interested. It's just nice sometimes to know that a few people out there other than dried up old university professors would like to hear what we've found out.'

'You haven't told Mr Oakley about the barrow yet, Ellie.'

'No, sorry—I was side-tracked and got onto my soap-box. It's a failing of mine. Well, Mr Oakley, I presume then that you know about the Bronze Age barrow near the cemetery sites.'

'Yes, it's still quite prominent in the landscape.'

'That's because the land it's on is useless for agriculture, and so the barrow escaped the attentions of the plough.'

'Presumably.'

'Definitely. Well, the barrow's pretty typical Late Bronze Age and we didn't expect it to reveal anything because—well, doubtless Mr Disvan has told you about the 1890 attack on it...'

'No, he hasn't actually.'

'No? Oh well, in line with the practices of the time, the Binscombe Barrow was one of about a dozen ransacked in the course of a summer's day by an Antiquarian Society from Hampstead. Their hired workmen simply dug a trench straight down through it whilst the members stood around and watched or ate a picnic. It was a common thing in those days—a pleasant day's pillaging for the educated well-to-do.'

'Did they find anything?'

'We don't know. As per normal, the expedition wasn't written up other than a very brief paragraph in *The Gentleman's Magazine*. If there was a burial or cremation burial in there, they must have taken the bones and/or pot, and God knows where they could be nowadays. All they left for posterity was a great backfilled hole.'

'That must be frustrating for you.'

'You get used to it. Future generations of archaeologists will probably feel the same about our efforts. Anyway, the point is that we've found that the barrow was re-used long after its creation and that there's a Roman double burial in one side—something the Victorian vandals missed.'

'And that's unusual is it?'

'Not desperately, but taken in conjunction with the Iron Age/Roman continuity in the main cemeteries, the whole site's quite a find.'

'I'm gratified to hear that,' said Mr Disvan, 'but where are the rest of your excavators?'

'They're mostly MSC, sorry, Manpower Services Commission, people or day volunteers, so they're not around in the evening. There's three other people from the university with me but... well, they've got other interests than coming down to meet the villagers.'

'And where do you fit into the group, Ellie?' I asked.

'Director, whip-cracker and sometime cook— which reminds me, I ought to be heading back to see what's on food-wise. Besides which I've got a lot of writing up to do.'

'Perhaps we could offer you a lift,' said Disvan. 'It's a tidy old trek up through the roads to the ridge. Twenty minutes walk for anyone.'

Ellie seemed very pleased to receive this offer.

'Ordinarily I wouldn't like to impose but...'

'Mr Oakley, your car is here, isn't it? You can drive us there can't you?'

I had a mere second in which to assert myself and resist this press-ganging before my hesitation would be detected and my churlishness revealed. As always the second passed and, long hard day and thirst notwithstanding, I agreed.

'That's very kind of you' she said.

'Not at all.'

I finished my drink, and a few minutes later we were driving through the centre of the Binscombe Estate out towards the wilder agricultural and wooded area that surrounded it. The path to the ridge was a mere sunken mud track off a minor road but was nominally negotiable to motor vehicles, although in parts perilously narrow and beset by trees. As I struggled with the problems it posed and pondered on the mud and scratches my car was accumulating, I heard Mr Disvan and Ellie chatting learnedly about the dig, the site, and its place within the lost past of Binscombe. Even at the best of times I would have had little to contribute to such a conversation and so, in between desperate hauling at the wheel and the piling on of gas or brake, I was content merely to listen in to snippets of their talk.

At length the car gamely took a very steep rise, at the top of which was a closed five-bar gate. Not far beyond, in a circle cleared of the bracken which grew all about, could be seen four or five tents, a large prefabricated wooden hut, and a patchwork of excavated areas. Above them, on the very apex of the ridge, loomed the dark elongated shape of the barrow. Plainly we had arrived. Ellie suddenly fell silent and there was a slight period of hesitation before she said, 'I'll just go and open the gate, then.'

'Okay, your door is unlocked.'

'Fine—right then.'

She left the car and sprinted over to the gate. The rope loop which held it shut took a time to disengage, and while she struggled with it she cast numerous glances into the thick mass of trees and bracken which came up close to the path on either side. Once it was free she hurried the gate forward and waved us on. Within a few seconds of me clearing the gap she had closed and fastened the gate and was in the car again.

'Is there some problem?' said Mr Disvan.

'Problem? No,' she replied, 'we're almost there, drive on.'

I duly covered the few hundred yards to the camp-site and halted the car on a reasonably level piece of ground.

'Thank you very much,' said Ellie, 'it was most kind of you. Come on over and meet the other full-timers. I'll rustle up a cup of cocoa or coffee for you.'

'That'd be nice,' said Mr Disvan, 'we'll take you up on that offer. Follow me, Mr Oakley, don't be shy.'

Up to that point, I'd been thinking in terms of a swift trip back down Binscombe's answer to the slalom in order to resume my interrupted visit to the Argyll. However, since we'd made it this far it seemed reasonable to accept the offer, even though Disvan's habit of speaking for me irked as before.

We followed Ellie to what was obviously the focal point of the camp: a large hearth of stacked bricks with a covering of corrugated iron over its top. Here, presumably, was where the meals were cooked and consumed. While Mr Disvan and I tried to make ourselves comfortable on the tree trunks which served as seats, Ellie put a kettle on to boil over a primus.

'It's humble, but it's home,' she said. 'At least for a while.'

Then, while we were sipping the resultant black coffee out of plastic cups, Ellie gave the hearth's iron roof several hard blows with a stick. The clanging noise thus produced caused a curious head to peer out of one of the nearby tents and look about to find the source of the disturbance. Obviously our arrival by car and subsequent chat had not been sufficient to rouse him or her.

'Visitors,' shouted Ellie, and the head nodded and then withdrew back into the tent.

'You'll have to excuse them—they're preoccupied,' she said.

'Them? I only saw one.'

'There's more.' She smiled as if at a private witticism. 'In every sense of the word.'

'It's a fine outlook you have here,' said Mr Disvan.

It was indeed. Below us the ridge fell away sharply and we had a clear and panoramic view of the rolling fields and lanes which led up to the start of Binscombe and the orderly, close packed streets beyond. A light mist was rising over the old glebe lands by the school and, in the distance, the sheen of Broadwater Lake was visible. The bird's farewell evening chorus from the trees on the slope provided a pleasing soundtrack, and we carried on silently taking in the scene set out before us for several moments.

Then the low roar and rumble of a forty-tonne juggernaut coping with the twists and turns of the Compton Road eventually reached us and broke the spell, dragging us back to the mundane world.

' "All the kingdoms of the world and the glory thereof",' Ellie said, smiling pleasantly and waving her arm towards the horizon.

'Pardon?'

'A joke. A quote I learnt at school.'

'It's Biblical, Mr Oakley,' said Mr Disvan as if to a slow but favoured child. 'Mr Oakley is the product of a strictly secular upbringing, Ellie. He'll not understand your allusion, I'm afraid.'

'Should I know it?' I asked.

'Probably not necessary,' Ellie replied. 'More coffee?'

'No thanks.'

'Hello,' said a soft voice from behind. Mr Disvan and I turned rapidly to see that Ellie's colleagues had silently joined us. She had been correct in saying that there were more—three in fact.

'Hello,' they repeated in unison.

'Dave, Ros and Jayney, I'd like you meet Mr Disvan and Mr Oakley from the village. You two, please meet Dave, Ros and Jayney.'

'Nice to meet you,' said Mr Disvan, rising and shaking hands with each.

'Likewise,' I added.

'Be careful,' said Ellie to her friends. 'Mr D and Mr O know a frightening amount about our trade.'

In Binscombe circles the three arrivals stood out somewhat. Dave had shoulder length, slicked back hair and wore a sizeable amount of make-up. Ros and Jayney were petite earth mother figures on whom the fashions of the sixties counter culture and a future post apocalypse age struggled for ascendancy. Heavy rings of eye shadow gave them a friendly, panda-ish look.

Even so, our greetings were none the less warm or genuine, for I had perforce gone beyond judging books by their covers, and Disvan was seemingly never disconcerted by anything or anyone.

Hand in hand, the three came to join us on a nearby tree trunk-cum-bench.

'Do you want to eat?' said Ellie.

'Maybe later,' replied Jayney.

'I'll get a fire going in the hearth then,' said Dave, and proceeded efficiently to do so.

In the event we stayed far longer than initially envisaged and shared the archaeologist's meal of beans and rice. Sitting round the blazing fire, with the barrow above us and the lights of Binscombe below, ultimately seemed very agreeable to me, and I relinquished any thoughts of returning to the Argyll. Mr Disvan got into a deep debate with the *ménage à trois* about the evidence for post-Roman social systems that could perhaps be derived from early Welsh legal codes and land deeds. Then he became even more popular when his meerschaum pipe was produced and shared round. The peculiar aroma it produced wafted over the hillside in competition with the wood smoke and added its dubious charms to the pleasant fragrance of the evening.

Since I could add nothing to the discussion described above and Ellie did not seem minded to join in, our little gathering split into two groups, one silent and one not. I noticed that whereas my gaze was relaxed and more or less undirected, Ellie was staring fixedly into the woods that surrounded the encampment on all sides other than that occupied by the barrow. She seemed more tense than the situation demanded or merited, and I assumed that some unpleasant recollection had occurred to her. In order to dispel this, and—okay—perhaps with some idea of establishing more intimate relations, I decided to strike up a conversation.

'I had no idea it was this pleasant on the ridge,' I said. 'It must be very easy to get to feel at home up here.'

'That's the whole problem,' she replied, her mood obviously unchanged by having her thoughts interrupted. 'It's far too easy to feel at home here.'

Mr Disvan appeared to have caught this answer and had broken off his talk, mid-sentence, to look intently at her.

'I don't suppose,' I asked, with little confidence in obtaining a positive response, 'that you'd care to clarify that remark?'

'You're right, Mr Oakley,' she said. 'I wouldn't care to even if I could.'

Mr Disvan swiftly rose to his feet.

'I think we'd best be going. Time is moving on and Mr Oakley has to work tomorrow, don't you? Doubtless we shall all meet again.'

* * *

In the event, Mr Disvan's prediction was fulfilled in very short order. The very next evening I noticed, upon my arrival, that once again Ellie and he were sitting out in the Argyll's garden. I fetched a drink and hastened to join them.

'Oh, hello, Mr Oakley,' she said. 'Nice to meet you again.'

'My sentiments exactly.'

'Be careful of Mr Oakley,' said Disvan, 'he's something of a charmer when he wants to be.'

'I'll bear it in mind,' Ellie replied, unimpressed. 'Incidentally, talking of charm or the lack of it, you two left very suddenly last night, didn't you? I hope it wasn't something I said.'

'No, of course not,' I replied.

'Not especially, no,' Disvan agreed—or at least partly agreed.

'Good. The thing is that I'm more of a city person myself, and being out in the country, amidst the trees and fields so to speak, tends to make me a bit broody—even anti-social sometimes. Hence my behaviour at the end yesterday.'

'How awful for you,' said Mr Disvan. 'Can't you get professional help to cure it?'

'Well,' Ellie replied, a little taken aback, 'it takes all sorts to make a world.'

'Oh yes, there is that saying.'

I decided to intervene before this exchange became barbed.

'Rest assured, Ellie, you gave no grounds for offence. As Mr Disvan said, I had to be up early for work and I'd forgotten. Anyway, have you made good progress today?'

'Not in archaeological terms, no, but in terms of my career, yes, I think I have.'

'How do you mean?'

'My study supervisor came down from the university to see me and visit the dig today. He's heard the word that, together with what I've already submitted and the results that this excavation will produce, my Ph.D. should sail through without a problem.'

'Congratulations, you must be very pleased.'

'Pleased and relieved, yes I am. I've invested five years hard work, not to mention the attendant poverty, in that doctorate, and the only alternative to having it passed that I'd be prepared to accept is death! Don't look so shocked Mr Disvan; I'm only joking. Probably.'

'What next?' I asked.

'Oh, the usual limbo, I should imagine. The dole in between odd archaeological commissions. Pouring over *The Times* and *Guardian* university appointments columns for years on end. Possibly a lectureship at the end of it if I'm lucky. So long as I don't have to get married and/or settle down I don't really mind.'

Disvan obviously didn't like this line of questioning and wanted to keep things specific.

'Is the entire doctorate to do with cemeteries, Ellie?' he asked.

'Yes, Romano-British ones to be specific, the later the better. Mind you, I've often dabbled back into the Iron Age if there's the slightest evidence for continuity.'

'As there is in the case of Binscombe.'

'Like there is here, as you say. Only here there's continuity to an extraordinary degree, which is pleasing. A sort of crowning glory to my researches, if you like.'

'Why did you choose cemeteries in particular?' asked Mr Disvan.

'Dunno—that's the honest answer. I just got interested in them early on, I suppose, had a few ideas, and felt like following them up. It's not everyone's idea of paradise when your foremost companions are the dead and gone, but it's better than filling in forms in a office. At least I think so.'

There seemed to be, at heart, a lot of truth in this, not least in relation to my own life, and I pondered on it as I went to fetch a fresh round of drinks from the bar. When I returned I found that, in my absence, the conversation had remained on much the same topic, shifting only slightly in location to the subject of the barrow on the ridge.

'No,' said Ellie in answer to a question of Mr Disvan's that I did not catch, 'we've left the burial alone. From what we saw when it was first revealed, the level of disturbance is so low, and the preservation of the remains so good, that I felt justified in leaving it so a specialist could do the full works. The original clothing, if any, may have left very subtle soil staining, for instance, which we mightn't pick up—things like that. I've got the evidence I want from the main cemeteries, so I won't be too disappointed if the barrow burials aren't up to expectations. If they are—if they're late Roman, say, it'll just be the cherry on the top.'

'Well then,' said Disvan, 'we wish you luck.'

'You can do better than that even. The specialist from the Institute in London is coming down on Friday. Why don't you both take the day off and come up to the dig? You can keep your fingers crossed for me and see what turns up at the same time.'

'I was hoping you'd offer that opportunity,' said Mr Disvan, 'but I didn't like to ask. I gladly accept.'

'What about you, Mr Oakley?'

'Won't we be in the way?'

'I wouldn't have asked you if I couldn't rely on you not to be.'

'Righto, it's a date. Expect us on Friday, then.'

'Good. Right, gentlemen, who's for more drinks?'

'Just a fruit juice for Mr Oakley,' said Disvan, 'he's got to drive you home later.'

I turned to look at Mr Disvan and he returned my gaze with beatific innocence, as if completely unaware that he was ordering my evening. Try as I might I could detect no mockery or guile.

'That's right,' I said slowly, 'so I have.'

* * *

It was very dark when we returned, but the path to the ridge was not so much of a problem the second time around. I knew which deep sloughs of permanent mud to avoid and which bushes in particular offered do or die resistance to a car's progress. Even so, all my concentration was required to prevent insurance-claim-worthy damage to the car's bodywork and therefore, once again, I failed to follow Mr

Disvan's and Ellie's conversation as we neared the camp. Nevertheless, despite my lack of attention, I noticed that as before, once the five-bar gate came into sight, Ellie lapsed into nervous silence and hesitated perceptibly before leaving the car to clear our way.

On this occasion the rope binding on the gate seemed to be more recalcitrant than before and Ellie struggled wildly to release it without effect.

'She's making a meal of that,' said Mr Disvan. 'I think I'll go and help her.'

Just as these words left his lips, Ellie stood stock still and stared hard into the trees and thickets on her left. She remained thus for a second or so, a horrified look on her face, before turning as if to run back to the car. A few steps into this sudden change of plan she stopped, obviously thought better of it, and returned to the gate. From the depths of one of the pockets of her Belstaff jacket she drew a large clasp knife, and with deft actions sawed asunder the offending rope loop. Kicking the gate open she raced back to the car and flung herself in.

'What is..?' I started to say, but Ellie pointed forward and shouted, in a voice not lightly to be contradicted, 'Go, go, go!'

I obliged by causing the car to leap forward just as fast as first gear would permit.

'Don't stop here,' she said. 'Go right up to the tents.'

'But we'll wake...'

'Just do it, please!'

'Okay, okay.'

We came to a halt, engine racing furiously, a mere few feet from the first tent. The headlights lit it up and roused, if the noise had not already done so, the three occupants.

'Thanks,' said Ellie, 'and sorry.'

She got out of the car and dived without further ado into what was presumably her tent, just as Dave's head emerged quizzically from his shared abode.

Mr Disvan and I emerged from the car feeling rather ridiculous and guilty. Ellie did not join us to lend support.

Dave looked at us as if at apprehended scrumpers. 'Can you offer any explanation for your behaviour?' he said. The public school tones were a surprise.

'Well...' I started, and then was glad for once that Mr Disvan took it upon himself to speak for me.

'To be absolutely honest, I'm afraid that we can't,' he said disarmingly.

'I see,' said Dave. 'Well, in that case I'll bid you goodnight—and drive carefully,' he added, withdrawing his head back into the tent and fastening the zip.

We were left alone, our feeling of stupidity undiminished. I reversed the car as quietly as one can on a silent hillside and, in a state of some puzzlement, we returned to the lights of Binscombe.

'What do you make of all that?' I said to Mr Disvan.

'I'm not sure, but we'll know when Ellie tells us herself tomorrow.'

'How can you be sure that she will?'

'Because,' he replied with certainty in his voice, 'her sense of propriety will make her.'

'We shall see,' I said doubtfully.

* * *

'I couldn't just leave it as it was,' said Ellie. 'I had to offer you some explanation.'

Mr Disvan gave me something approaching an 'I told you so' look.

'Besides which,' she continued, 'I think I need your

advice.'

We were once again sitting out in the Argyll's beer garden enjoying the mellow evening sunshine. Ellie looked even more incongruous among us than usual, for the majority of the clientele were, on this occasion, dressed in formal black and a few sported black armbands, whereas she adhered to her customary paramilitary school of fashion. I suspected, however, that her evident unease was not due to any sense of being incorrectly attired.

She had been waiting for some time before our arrival back from the memorial service and wake that had arisen from Stan, the local policeman's, suicide just over a week before. We briefly explained the reason for our sombre garb and then, as was fast becoming the custom, took our drinks into the garden.

'It's a more suitable and private place for the dispensing of advice,' Mr Disvan said.

There was a standard family (father, mother, boy and girl) of trippers already in occupation of our normal table and so, to avoid being overheard, we had to sit at the far end of the garden by Lottie's flower beds and the kiddies' swing and sand pit. At one point it looked as if the trippers' offspring were minded to come and make use of these facilities, but Disvan managed to catch their eye and they revised their plan so as to stay close to mum and dad.

Ellie looked suspiciously about her and felt the need for a sip at her drink and a drag from her cigarette before commencing whatever she had to tell us.

'This isn't going to be easy for me,' she said by way of warning.

'Perhaps I can assist you, then,' said Mr Disvan. 'What is it that you can see or hear in the woods by the gate?'

Ellie looked at him keenly.

'It's that obvious, is it?'

'Fairly.'

'I suppose my actions the last couple of nights haven't been all that normal or subtle. Okay then, you've guessed my secret. The next big question is whether you'll believe me.'

'You haven't told us what the problem is yet,' I said.

'No, that's true. It's just that I'm naturally reluctant to get around to revealing it. The problem is, gentlemen, that I hear voices in the wood—or one voice, to be quite specific.'

'And this occurs when you're by the gate does it?' asked Mr Disvan.

'Generally, but not always. I've heard it when I've been near other parts of the woods.'

'And what does it say?'

'To start with it was just like a sighing—a man's sigh when he's expressing a longing for something. Then it developed into a whisper saying things that were indistinct, but even so I still ignored it. I told myself it was just the wind in the trees or some defect in my hearing. But then last night, at the gate, the voice was quite clear—and it was calling for me.'

'In what way?'

'Just by saying my name: "Ellie...Ellie..." it was saying. It wanted me to come to it.'

'And it was a man's voice, you say?'

'In origin, perhaps, but it sounded as if was coming from a million miles away. It really was a vile, cold voice, Mr Disvan!'

'Well, don't distress yourself anew Ellie. It's broad daylight now and you're in company.'

'That hasn't prevented it from happening before. One of the first occasions I heard it was when I was doing some grid-planning in the lunch hour.

Suddenly all the birds rose out of the woods and flew off in a crowd and, in the silence they left behind, I heard the voice whispering to me. Oh no, Mr Disvan, daylight's no safeguard, I'm afraid.'

Once upon a time I would have doubted, made discreet remarks about mental stability, and sought rational explanations. Now, after years of Binscombe residence, I found within myself the ability to accept the unlikely as quite probable—Ellie's story included.

'In that case,' I said, in an attempt to be both practical and helpful, 'assuming it's not something awry with your ears or to do with the wind through the branches, there's a ready solution to your problem.'

'And what might that be, Mr Oakley?' said Disvan looking at me with interest.

'It's that as far as possible you keep out of earshot of the woods or, if you must work alongside them, use one of those Walkman things. That way you won't hear whatever the voice might care to say. Also, leave the gate open and unfastened if you leave the site. I'm more than willing to give you a lift back in the evenings, and we can drive straight on and drown anything your friend's got to whisper with the noise of the car.'

Mr Disvan nodded his approval. 'Given that an explanation for your voice is unlikely and that your stay on the ridge is only temporary, Mr Oakley's proposals have a lot of sense in them,' he said.

'Thank you' I replied. 'After all, as Mr Disvan says, it's not as if you'll be there for ever, is it? How much longer do you really need to stay?'

'Two, maybe three weeks,' said Ellie.

'There you are then. That's not too long a time to display a little eccentricity—especially in the context of the rest of your team.'

'It's very nice of you to believe me, both of you,' Ellie said warmly, although apparently little cheered by my suggestions.

'Here in Binscombe, it's not so hard to credit,' I replied. 'For instance, one person we knew heard...'

I intercepted Mr Disvan's gaze and, because of the note of caution contained therein, dried up immediately.

'Mr Oakley means that we realise you're a person of integrity and so we're obliged to believe what you say. Isn't that so, Mr Oakley?'

'That's right...' I concurred weakly.

'Well, thank you anyway,' Ellie continued. 'I was afraid you'd think I was cracking up but, all things considered, I don't think I am. Not yet anyway. I appreciate what you've suggested, Mr Oakley but unfortunately your measures wouldn't be any help.'

'How do you mean?'

'Well, for example, you said to stay clear of the woods, out of earshot, didn't you?'

'Yes, that was one of the things.'

'I thought so. Sadly you see, there isn't anywhere on the site out of range of the voice if it wants to reach me. I've even heard it while we were sitting round the campfire and Ros and Jayney were talking to me. However, I can't go around with a Walkman on, blaring away all the time, even if I could afford one. It wouldn't be practical—or professional for that matter.'

'Okay,' I said, 'but at least you could leave the gate open so you wouldn't have to linger there to unfasten it each time you passed.'

'No again. There was terrible trouble this morning as it was, what with the fastening being found sawed off and so on. The road to the ridge is privately owned. We can use it in moderation but one of the strictest stipulations that the owner made was that all gates were to be kept closed.'

'Why?'

'I don't know.'

'I do,' said Mr Disvan. 'That land's owned by a man called Griffiths and he's got a real mania for tidiness. He drove his wife mad, he did, following her round straightening piles of magazines and looking for dust. I well recall their wedding and the rumpus over the confetti. They had to get in extra police from Goldenford.'

I interrupted a potential stream of Disvan remembrances and brought the conversation back to the matter in hand.

'Well then, Ellie, I'm afraid that all my good ideas are brought to nought.'

'It seems so, yes.'

'One thing,' said Mr Disvan, 'what exactly did you mean by saying it was too easy to feel at home on the ridge?'

'Just that, Mr D. Despite the voice, despite everything, I more and more feel that I belong up there. I don't want to feel that way, but it just keeps on growing.'

'That is worrying,' said Disvan. 'You've no Binscombe blood in you, unless I'm very much mistaken.'

'No, I shouldn't think so. My family, such as it is, are from all over.'

'How much longer did you say you are staying here?'

'Two to three weeks.'

Mr Disvan fixed her with one of the most earnest and impressive looks in his extensive repertoire.

'Don't make it any longer,' he said.

'I shan't, don't worry.'

'Good. In the meanwhile I advise you to ignore what the voice says to you. Just try to live with it but don't listen to it. You can borrow my Walkman if you like. I've also got one of those portable compact disc players. It's very impressive.'

'Thanks anyway, but no thanks.'

'Just as you wish.'

'A lift home would be more than welcome, though.'

'It would be our pleasure,' said Mr Disvan.

'Absolutely' I agreed.

Accordingly, in due course, I conveyed Ellie home. As we approached the infamous gate I turned the radio on loud while Mr Disvan disembarked to clear our path. The sounds of Little Richard pounding his inimitable way through 'Tutti Fruiti' percolated from the car into the silent woods, raucously drowning out, I hoped, anything Ellie's voice might wish to express. Within a brief moment Mr Disvan rejoined us and we were on our way. In deference to the sleep or other activities of the ménage I halted a little way off from the tents and turned the radio right down.

'Here we are, then,' I said, turning round to speak to Ellie in the back seat. 'How was that?'

Her face contained an eloquent answer to my question. She was pointing, plainly horrified, at the radio.

'Can't you hear it?' she said. 'It keeps breaking in to the song!'

Disvan and I listened intently but could discern nothing other than that which the artist intended.

'Oh my God,' Ellie cried almost panic-stricken, 'it says—'

And then she fainted.

* * *

'Feeling better now?' asked Mr Disvan.

'Yes thank you, very much better,' Ellie replied.

'How did you explain to Dave and co about us

carrying you in?' I asked.

'That was very simple. I said I was dead drunk. Knowing me as they do, it had the ring of truth. I'd have said anything rather than let it be known that I'd fainted.'

'There's no shame in it,' said Mr Disvan. 'You'd had a bad shock.'

'You don't know the half of it. But even so, fainting just isn't my image. Where did you say that villa was, Mr Disvan?'

Ellie obviously wanted the subject of the voice left alone. Disvan obliged by pointing out once again the position of one of the two Roman farms which had constituted, a civilisation ago, the Binscombe of the day, and whose one-time inhabitants presumably rested in the cemetery on the ridge.

The Friday had dawned promisingly clear and bright and developed into a fine sunny day that a persistent breath of wind saved from becoming too warm. Mr Disvan and I met by arrangement early on, and after breakfast in a café we had driven up to the dig. The 'Bone Specialist' from London was already there, supervising Ros and Jayney as they uncovered the barrow burials. Ellie, having set the rest of the diggers to work, was at something of an anticipatory loose end and was thus free to give us a tour round the site.

Mr Disvan made intelligent and incisive comments about the finds and holes we were shown, and I nodded sagely at what seemed the right moments. It all looked very professional to me, but the repeated sight of pottery and bone fragments and alleged soil features that I found invisible soon began to pall. I was pleased, therefore, when Dave rattled on the hearth's tin roof to signify it was lunch time, and Ellie suggested we fetch our sandwiches from the site hut and sit lower down on the hillside to eat them.

Behind us, the motley crew of government-enlisted youths and genteel volunteers sprawled around the hearth area munching their food and listening to Capital Radio on a transistor. Carried away by enthusiasm, the Specialist and Ros and Jayney worked on.

'It was an enclosed courtyard type villa by the middle fourth century,' continued Mr Disvan, ' very much in the continental style, really, which adds to the theory that there were a lot of rich Gallo-Romans coming over to Britannia at that time to escape the social troubles in their province.'

'The *Bacaudae* you mean?' said Ellie.

'That's right. Bands of brigands and revolutionaries and army deserters. Anyway, this villa was unusual in that it later had a defensive wall and rampart built around it.'

'How do you know that?' Ellie asked.

'How? Well, it was in the 1960 excavation report by the Goldenford Archaeological Society.'

'No it wasn't. I've read it. They were digging in advance of an expansion of the council estate and they didn't have time to excavate anything other the building itself.'

'Oh well, I must have seen it in the report of Janaway's dig in 1908.'

'No, I don't think so, I've read that as well.'

'How strange,' said Disvan hurriedly, 'I could have sworn I read it somewhere. Anyway, getting back to what you told us last week, have you heard anything more of your voice?'

'Not the voice, no. Well, maybe some mumbling on the very edge of my hearing but nothing like... like when I fainted.'

'You don't want to explain about that by any chance, do you?' said Mr Disvan.

'No, it's too personal. However... there is something I can tell you about.'

'What's that?'

'I think the voice or whatever it is has taken shape.'

'How do you know that?' I asked.

'It sounds quite an innocent story when I tell it.'

'Go ahead, even so,' said Disvan.

'It's just that I was lying awake in my tent a couple of nights ago—I've not been sleeping well for obvious reasons—when someone came marching along and stood outside.'

'What's so strange about that?' I queried.

'Look at where my tent is.'

We did as we were asked, and saw that on one side the thick bracken which surrounded the cleared camp site grew chest high.

'And the footsteps came from the side where the bracken is?' I hazarded.

'You've guessed it. No one could walk at a steady normal pace through that. It'd be hard work for a strong man to walk even a few paces, and he wouldn't be able to stride along like the footsteps I heard.

'No, you're right,' said Disvan. 'What did you do?'

'I stayed put, terrified out of my mind, until the sun came up and I heard the footsteps walk away.'

'That was wise, I'm thinking.'

'Did you inspect the bracken in the morning?' I asked.

'Yes—very cautiously, but I did. There was a line of dead and blackened plants leading back into the woods.'

'Leading where?'

'Nowhere. Dave followed the trail for me, and apparently it just petered out after a hundred feet or so.'

There was silence for a moment (if one discounts

Capital Radio and the sound of eating) while we considered this story. Disvan then turned to speak to Ellie.

'I think you should leave here. Leave now and never come back.'

Ellie looked out over the panorama of Binscombe and beyond. When she replied she sounded listless and resigned.

'I can't. You're probably right, but I just can't leave now. There's too much tied up for me in this dig. I'm very scared by what's going on, but somehow I'm not so scared as perhaps I should be. It's a strange sensation, but I think I feel less and less threatened by whatever it is.'

'Therein lies the danger,' said Mr Disvan, 'because if you don't—'

Jayney came racing along and interrupted what Disvan was about to say.

'Ellie, come and look,' she said, 'the burials are really amazing!'

'Marvellous,' said Ellie, instantly her old self once again. 'Come on, gents, follow me and see my doctorate come to fruition!'

Mr Disvan shook his head in dismay, but did as he was told without trying to complete his warning.

A few minutes brisk walk took us to the top of the ridge and the barrow. Dave, Ros and the Specialist were huddled around a neat rectangular excavation in the barrow's side and were gesturing excitedly. Our approach was heard and the 'bone man', as Ellie had termed him, came to meet us. He was a thick-set young man whose eyes contained an unhappy, dangerous energy, placated, for the moment, by the pleasure of his discovery. An ancient and baggy black woolly hat distinguished his pseudo-martial dress from all the other archaeologists I'd so far met.

'It's a beauty, Ellie,' he said. 'Two inhumations, man and a woman, articulation and dentition practically complete in both cases, so we'll get age and any pathological indicators, no trouble. There's no sign of a coffin and no trace of soil staining from a shroud that I can detect, but there are grave goods—fantastic stuff too—just right for your purposes.'

'What are they?' Ellie said.

'Coins over the eyes.'

'Pagan Roman then.'

'Yep. Pretty late, I think, as well.'

'Great.'

'And there's a gold ring. Looks like there might be an inscription on it.'

'Fantastic. Let me have a look.'

We all gathered round to survey the find as described. Two skeletons lay on the ground, all the soil skilfully cleared away from them, as if they had been beached there during the Great Flood. Their involuntary grin greeted the rays of the sun for the first time in perhaps fifteen hundred years, and its light shone brightly off their skulls and the large golden coins resting neatly in their eye sockets.

Ellie knelt beside them and with a tweezer device gently picked up the coins one by one.

'A gold *solidus* of Honorius and... another of the same for this one.'

'That's the male,' said the bone man.

'And a... don't know, and a *trimus* of Magnus Maximus for this one.'

'The female,' the woolly-hatted man added unnecessarily.

'About as late as you can get and still be Roman,' Dave announced.

'And very prosperous people too,' Jayney said.

'Yes,' Ellie concurred smiling. 'Prosperous enough

probably to be the top people in an off the track area like this. Anyway, the people who buried them made sure they had enough money to pay the ferryman so they wouldn't need to come back for more.'

'Note the discrimination against the woman, though,' said Dave. 'Lesser value coins for her.'

'It's noted, Dave,' Ellie replied. 'Now, let's have a look at that ring.'

She leant over what we now knew to be the male remains and extracted a small, plain looking gold ring which was loosely located on a phalange of what had been a right hand. While brushing it with a whisk, Ellie's smile broadened even more.

'Yes, there is an inscription, you're right. Any Latinists here?'

'Sorry,' said Dave, 'coins and the occasional milestone are about my limit, I'm afraid.'

I did not feel it necessary to announce my ignorance since it was presumably taken for granted, and a quiet born of frustration came over us.

'Ah well,' said Ellie, obviously disappointed, 'It'll have to wait till we can phone somebody.'

Mr Disvan, apparently having held his peace while he considered the matter, then spoke.

'That may not be necessary. I have some facility with that language.'

'Great,' said Ellie straightening up and holding the tweezer-held ring close to Disvan's face. 'What, if anything, do you make of it?'

Mr Disvan screwed up his features and peered at the ring. His head followed the inscription round as he inwardly read it.

'Well,' he said at length, 'it's tiny script, and much abbreviated: but the sense is:

HELENA: VOX MEA VENIET QUOCUMQUE ES

which broadly translated means:

ELLEN: MY VOICE SHALL COME TO
YOU WHEREVER'

'Wow,' said the bone man, 'that's pretty weird isn't it, Ellie? Ellie, what's the matter?'

The person in question was now quite oblivious to our presence and was staring from ring to grave and back again as if at approaching nemesis. The archaeologists were puzzled as to what precisely was happening, but could see that somehow Mr Disvan knew more about it than they.

'What's the problem, Mr Disvan?' asked Dave.

Disvan ignored him and instead spoke to Ellie in a tone that was half admonition and half bitter regret.

'I told you to go, didn't I?' he said.

* * *

That summer saw a run of fine evenings when clouds were nigh absent and the sun warmed and cheered rather than oppressed. One such evening, a few days after our visit to the dig, Ellie came once again to visit us at the Argyll. Mr Disvan seemed to have anticipated her arrival since, contrary to normal practise, he suggested we take our drinks in the garden and join the one or two family groups already there. When Mr Wessner and Mr Patel asked if they might join us he politely declined—sorry, no, he said, we may have a guest and the conversation might be personal-like. Mr Wessner and Mr Patel said they quite understood.

A few minutes after seating ourselves Ellie arrived. She seemed both pleased and abashed to see us.

'How are you settling in at the Constantine's?' Mr Disvan asked when she had fetched a drink and joined us.

'Couldn't be better. I'm being killed with kindness.'

'Good, I told you you'd be made very welcome.'

'It makes a pleasant change from my normal habitat of tents, squats and grotty B&B places,' Ellie added. 'I'm well overdue for a spot of pampering—good food prepared for me, clean sheets and that sort of thing.'

The explanation for the above conversation lies in the post mortem held on the events of the previous Friday. In the evening Disvan and I, Ellie, the *ménage* and the bone man had adjourned to the Argyll, nominally to celebrate the day's find, now safely covered again. By prearrangement, I fielded the archaeologists' conversation and occupied them with increasingly banal questions while Disvan and Ellie went off in a huddle to discuss matters of more import. The upshot of their sometimes heated debate was a compromise solution in which Ellie refused to abandon the dig but agreed she should minimise the time spent there. To this end, Mr Disvan found her lodgings in the house of Dorothy and Esther Constantine, two spinster sisters of his acquaintance, where she now slept and dined.

For all the doubtless lavish hospitality being showered upon her by the Constantines, Ellie did not look well. Her eyes were surrounded by dark rings that resembled the effects produced by Ros and Jayney's cosmetics, and her cheeks were sunken. While nominally at repose, her fingers twitched and fiddled with anything to hand.

'And how is everything else?' I asked, pretending that her condition was not already sufficient answer to my question.

Ellie either ignored or did not hear me and, draining her drink, she looked up to stare at Mr Disvan.

'I've been thinking,' she said, 'and I've come to the conclusion that you're right.'

Disvan shrugged his shoulders.

'I take no pleasure in your agreement but, at the same time, I'm glad you've decided to face facts, however strange they might seem. It's for the best that you should go but we shall miss you. Shan't we, Mr Oakley?'

'What? Oh yes, we shall of course. Er... excuse me, but what exactly is going on?'

Ellie favoured me with the arresting look she had just bestowed on Disvan.

'Its getting worse, as Mr Disvan said it would. The voice is loud and clear now. When I walk to the site in the morning and back again in the evening it calls to me. All the way through the woods it never stops. He—for it is a he, that much is obvious—has become quite eloquent in the last few days.'

'What does he say?'

Ellie mimicked in a quavering, loud whisper, ' "Waiting for you, waiting for you... for so long, for so long" or "Another world here in the woods for us, for us... and it lasts for ever, for ever..." and other such phrases. Sometimes he just laughs and I can hear a woman's voice screaming or weeping.'

'How can you bear it?'

'Good question. Quite frankly I don't know, but I do know that I've had enough. You see, the worse thing is that while one part of me is frightened and revolted another, less conscious, part is relaxed and passive in an almost... well, erotic sort of way. You know—that sort of anticipatory tingle you sometimes get just beforehand.'

'Quite,' replied Mr Disvan abruptly.

Ellie said nothing more for a little while being obviously deep in thought. We left her to her reflections, thinking this to be the kindest thing to do, although Disvan watched her with great care. At length she lifted her head again and met Mr Disvan's gaze.

'It's me, isn't it,' she said slowly. 'It's me or a one-time me in that grave, isn't it?'

'It rather looks like that, I'm afraid,' Disvan answered calmly.

'Somehow I escaped, perhaps a long time ago, and now I've come back—or been drawn back, maybe. Remember what it said on that ring!'

'Since Saturday it has rarely been out of my mind, Ellie.'

The note of alarm in Ellie's voice heightened as her thoughts raced ahead. 'And from what I've heard—across the gulf of years—I don't think it was a happy marriage; not happy at all. I think that he flourishes in the cold of the grave and wants me back to be his wife there, to hold me prisoner like he did in life!'

'This could well be so,' agreed Disvan as if agreeing that the weekend might be warm or Arsenal might win the cup.

Ellie slammed her glass down on the table, alarming the other occupants of the beer garden.

'Well,' she shouted in anger, 'he shan't have me! I'm going and I'm not coming back. Tomorrow morning I'm going!'

A sudden burst of wind came from nowhere sending everyone scuttling to secure their drinks and possessions from being blown away. Mr Disvan's Panama hat went flying and a sun parasol over one table took to the air in unmanned flight. Ellie's hair was lifted up and alternately played wildly about her face or streamed straight back. She seemed to be concentrating on something other than the uproar around her and, to my surprise, great rolling tears began to slip from her eyes.

The wind then ceased as abruptly as it started.

'I don't care what you say,' Ellie sobbed, 'I'm still going.'

* * *

It had been agreed that Mr Disvan and I would settle up things for Ellie and explain her sudden departure with some plausible lie. I took yet another day off work and as the church clock struck ten (signifying it was circa 9:45) I met Mr Disvan outside the Argyll and drove us both to the excavation site. On our way we were obliged to pull over to allow a police car and an ambulance, both with their sirens and flashing lights on, to speed past us.

'Another family dispute in the estate, I expect,' said Disvan. 'Either that or the council trying to evict someone—probably the Abbott tribe again.'

For once, however, one of Disvan's predictions, although based on his seemingly omniscient knowledge of Binscombe, proved to be incorrect. As we made our way up the track to the ridge, there was every sign that someone had immediately preceded us—in large vehicles, such as a police car or an ambulance. This proved to be the case, and when we came upon the site through the already opened five-bar gate, it was to see said vehicles, their beacons still in operation, parked as close to the barrow as safety would permit.

Abandoning the car, we made haste to join the small crowd that was milling around the ambulance. I saw the *ménage*, two policemen and some MSC lads removing a large wooden structure that had inexplicably come to be on the side of the barrow. The 'bone man', as we knew him, was also there directing other

146

people who were in the burial trench itself.

As we drew near and made our way through the mob, the ambulance men finished loading an occupied stretcher into their vehicle and then drove off back down the hill at reckless speed.

Having disposed of the strange wooden object, the senior of the two policemen was having strong words or, more accurately, a strong monologue with Dave, who was weeping bitterly and ignoring his questioner completely. Ros and Jayney, one either side of him like book ends, were attempting to comfort the distraught archaeologist.

The policeman gesticulated wildly once more and then gave up in frustration. Following the direction of his arm I saw that the site hut had somehow been beheaded and that the puzzling wooden structure now lying by the side of the barrow was the hut's one-time roof. A horrible suspicion began to form in my mind.

Our approach was now audible even over the general furore, and the peeved look on the policemen's faces eased as they turned to inspect the new arrivals.

'Ah, Mr Disvan,' said one, 'good morning to you.'

'Morning, Alan. Morning, Desmond. What's going on?'

'Difficult to say. I can't get no sense out of these weirdoes. An accident caused by appalling safety standards, that much is plain, though.'

'Who's been hurt?' Disvan asked.

'Young girl. The one you've been taking a drink or two with lately.'

'How badly?'

'Bad as you can get. Her head's split. She'll be DOA.'

'Pardon?'

'Dead on arrival.'

'I see. Thank you, Alan. Look, perhaps I can assist you here; I'm acquainted with these people.'

'By all means, Mr Disvan, carry on.'

'Thank you.'

Mr Disvan crossed over to Dave and placed his hand on his shoulder.

'Hello, Dave' he said. 'I'm very sorry about what happened. Do you think you could tell me about it?'

Dave regained control of his emotions and answered in a level voice.

'Yeah, I'm all right now. It was when we were taking photographs of the burials. Someone opened the site hut door, there was a sudden almighty blast of wind and the roof blew off. I just don't understand that because I put it together myself—it should have been as firm as a rock...'

'Well, it wasn't, was it,' said a policeman, 'and furthermore...'

Mr Disvan waved him to silence. 'Carry on, Dave' he said gently.

'Well, it flew over here and we didn't see it coming because we had our backs to it and... it hit Ellie on the head—she was crouching over the burials you see—and there must have been some nails protruding from the roof because... Anyway, it hit her first and the rest of us were able to duck or roll underneath its path. Ellie got carried forward and pushed onto the graves and buried underneath the damn thing. We lifted it off but... there was nothing we could do to help her.'

'What was she doing here?' I asked.

The archaeologists looked at me in surprise.

'Why shouldn't she be here?' said the bone man. 'She came here every day, as you well know.'

'Of course. It's just that we were under the impression that... she'd been called away. We'd come up here to explain that to you.'

'Really?' the bone man continued. 'She didn't mention it to me when I came down from London and called at her lodgings this morning.'

'Why did you do that?' asked Mr Disvan.

'To pick up the coins and the ring which Ellie had in her safe keeping so we could do some extra pictures. The first lot didn't come out for some reason. There were some very odd effects of the light in them.'

'I warrant that this lot will be the same,' Disvan commented quietly.

The bone man looked at him sceptically.

'Don't see why—conditions were perfect. Anyhow, we had to have some decent pics before the burials were taken up, because without them Ellie's report would have been a bit of a laughing stock. And, for the pictures, I required the grave goods and Ellie to supervise. Actually, now you come to mention it, maybe Ellie was a bit reluctant to come up here with me. I put that down to the incident at the faculty Christmas party when I was a bit tipsy, but in view of what you say perhaps she did have an appointment elsewhere. That was Ellie all over—never able to delegate or back out of anything. It was one of her strengths.'

'There is also a strength in knowing when to back down,' said Mr Disvan solemnly.

'Don't understand what you mean, old boy,' said the bone man.

The policemen, local men both, winced at such unwarranted familiarity with Disvan.

'No, I don't suppose you do,' Mr Disvan agreed.

'Anyhow,' the specialist continued unabashed, 'it's all very, very sad...'

Mr Disvan and I nodded prematurely before hearing the bone man out.

'... the female burial is completely smashed,' he continued, 'and the male's is so messed up that it's not worth removing now. Worst of all, the ring seems to have vanished off the face of the earth.'

* * *

'Come, come,' said the coroner, 'there must be someone to take responsibility for this poor girl's remains.'

A policeman, unknown to me, rose and addressed the court.

'I'm afraid not,' he said. 'Parents divorced fifteen years ago, present whereabouts of father unknown, mother now remarried and resident in New Zealand, no other family known. The mother was notified and she has written to the Court, sir and she says...'

He took up an air mail letter and read stentoriously:

' "Please make such arrangements as you see fit for burial or cremation and after deduction of due expenses thereof please forward any remaining funds to..." And she appends her address, sir.'

'I see, I see,' the coroner said frostily. 'So much for ties of blood. Right then, we'd better do as bidden and act as we see fit. Is there a representative of the girl's university here?'

The junior lecturer who'd given evidence earlier rose and, obviously embarrassed, said that he had no authority... would need to refer... and so on.

Clearly pained by this travesty, Mr Disvan stood up.

'I will undertake to arrange for the deceased's funeral if the court so pleases.'

'I see, well, we're obliged to you, Mr...'

'Disvan.'

'And what was your connection to the deceased,

Mr Disvan?'

'Friend and advisor.'

'Is there anyone in court who can vouch for this?'

Rising as one, as they did in all other things, Dave, Ros and Jayney said that Mr Disvan had spoken the truth.

'Ah, thank you' said the Coroner regarding them with neutral curiosity.

'I can further attest to Mr Disvan's statement,' said the policeman known to me as Alan, who had also given evidence earlier.

'Good. Very well, let it be so recorded. Mr Disvan, kindly see the usher after this hearing in order that the formalities can be observed and the relevant papers signed. This court will rise.'

The usher, when we duly came to meet him, wrongly thought us to be a sympathetic audience for a well polished sermon on the rootless, existential nature of modern youth with particular reference to the case just heard. 'Take my daughter,' he said, 'please!' He concluded his case by saying, 'A clever girl her age ought to have a husband who'd take care of her remains.'

Mr Disvan smiled and said, 'Well, it's funny you should say that because...' before I bustled him away.

* * *

Aside from the Reverend Jagger and the corpse, Mr Disvan and I were the only people present at the cremation. The *ménage* promised to attend but failed to do so, presumably being archaeologically occupied elsewhere now that the Binscombe dig was finished. Similarly, the rumoured representative from the university was conspicuous by his or her absence. After a few short words on the brevity and uncertainty of life by the rector, and a taped hymn, Ellie's remains trundled off into the depths of the crematorium and, in their present form, out of the world.

We returned a while later and collected the ashes in the plastic urn provided.

'What now?' I asked.

'To the ridge, of course,' Mr Disvan replied as if stating the blindingly obvious.

'Do you intend, God forbid, what I think you intend?'

'That rather depends on what you're thinking.'

'I'm thinking that you propose to bury Ellie's ashes next to the male burial in the barrow.'

'Then you think right.'

'You can't!'

'On the contrary, I must. Such an ending is obviously ordained.'

'Nonsense.'

'No, not nonsense. Consider, Mr Oakley, the fact that Ellie's accident spoilt the human remains to such an extent that the archaeologists left them in place. Further consider the fact that the ring was never found. Everything that has been permitted to happen points to one conclusion, and we would be incorrect to act against it. No, Mr Oakley, there are times when one must move with the tide of events.'

'Even if the tide is wrong?'

'It's not given to us to see the outcome of all things. Considerations of ultimate right and wrong can stretch beyond the perspective of a single human lifetime. It's a matter of trust, you see.'

'In what?'

'If you don't know, I can't tell you.'

'But for heaven's sake, Mr Disvan, it's not what Ellie would have wanted, is it?.'

'Can you be so sure about that? Despite all that

she said to us that final time in the Argyll, she still went to the ridge the very next morning of her own free will.'

'To supervise pictures so her report could be completed.'

'Maybe—superficially, perhaps, but I can't believe she'd forgotten the risk so quickly. Remember that she spoke to us of her growing feeling of belonging up there. I think she realised that if it was not her that was rejoined it would be some descendent of hers. If not in this life, then in some other.'

'Is that what you thought, that there was no escape for her?'

'It was.'

'Why didn't you tell her?'

'It's hardly good news to rush to impart to someone. I thought she might escape the call for the duration of her lifetime, so I kept my ideas to myself. Clearly however, Ellie came to the same conclusion of her own accord—perhaps thinking it through that night after she left us. I think that at the last moment, leaning over the double burial with the ring in her hand, she accepted what was to come and the hut roof plighted their troth for a second time—with her permission.'

I thought about this for some while, and cursed the world. Then we set off in my car, taking Ellie on her final journey, to reunite the long parted couple.

The Will to Live

My first meeting with Terence the solicitor was in the course of one of his apparently regular, if infrequent, evening visitations to the Argyll. It was, by the merest of coincidences, the anniversary of Mr Bolding's disappearance and, spotting the memorial drink standing on the bar, Terence seized the opportunity to outrage local sensibilities by striding up to it and taking a sip.

'Bolding doesn't need it any more, does he?' he roared in a hoarse, dusty voice. 'Not as much as me, anyway, haw, haw, haw.'

His ostentatious arrival by Rolls Royce, much heralded by the trumpeting of its horn and concert pitch quadraphonic sound, and his brash eruption into the Argyll, had already done little to endear him to the clientele. The sacrilegious treatment of Bolding's drink and general behaviour thereafter completed the process of alienation.

Turning his back on the bar and placing his elbows upon it, Terence slowly surveyed the assembled company.

'Well, yokels,' he said with a joyless smirk, 'how is everything in your little world?'

Terence the solicitor was an extremely tall, extremely thin and extremely cadaverous man of perhaps forty years of age. The effect of his fine, well cut suit was offset by the pale angularity of his features and a certain unhealthy tautness to his skin. He put me in mind of a stringy, plucked bird clad in human clothes, or perhaps one of the featherless and blind chicks that you find fallen out of nests. Yet, despite these unfortunate likenesses, he seemed strangely familiar to me, although I could not at present place the association.

His companion, a hard eyed, beautiful woman of uncertain years, tittered at his remark and, by way of an obvious effort of will, snuggled up affectionately to him. In definite contrast to the other ladies present, she wore circulation-threatening leather trousers and a shimmering, scarlet blouse. Looking closely at this exotic creature and arriving eventually at her face, I noticed a curious tiredness there. Simultaneously, Terence looked down proprietarily at her and said in what I took to be a mock comforting tone, 'Yes, darling, it is a bit of a dump, but we needn't stay long.'

'If you don't like it, you know what you can bloody well do, don't you,' said the landlord, advancing along the length of the bar like a galley at ram speed.

Terence the solicitor turned to face him smiling sweetly.

'I beg your pardon?' he said.

The landlord stopped dead in his tracks, all his former confidence and certainty fled.

'Well... I won't have you running this place down in front of me like that. It's my home and my livelihood.'

'Of course it is, my dear man,' Terence replied, 'and I wouldn't dream of deprecating it—that means running it down, by the way. We think the Argyll is terribly quaint, don't we, Cheryl—just like Binscombe as a whole.'

Cheryl, as we now knew her to be, giggled again.

'Okay, then,' said Terence, licking his lips, 'what shall we have to drink?'

He leant over the bar to study the serried rows of bottles there, and Lenin the dog, who had been sleeping soundly on the floor up to this point, caught sight of him for the first time. The Alsatian let out a terrible yelp and, after running to the cellar door, pawed at it in an expression of desire to escape. The noisy canine protest did not cease until Lottie answered his pleas and set him free from our company.

'That dog's dangerous,' said Terence angrily. 'It's hysterical.'

'No, he's not,' the landlord replied; 'he's just particular about the company he keeps.'

We all smiled at this rejoinder, and probably sensing this, even if he did not see it, Terence decided to ignore the matter and to press on to regain lost ground.

'I don't suppose you do cocktails, do you?'

'You suppose right,' said the landlord.

This response surprised me for, it seeming appropriate given the heat of the evening, I had ordered and was currently consuming a Moscow Mule prepared by the landlord not ten minutes before.

'No?' Terence continued. 'On reflection I wonder why I bothered to ask—cocktails are perhaps a trifle sophisticated. Very well, we'll have a large dry martini each. With ice and lemon.'

'And a cherry on a stick, if you so wis,h' said the landlord.

'Yes, we do so wish, thank you so much.'

At this point, Mr Patel obviously felt that our natural hospitality had been imposed upon enough. Given that his daily employment was immigration control at Heathrow, it may be that experience had made him less inclined to suffer taunts than most, but even so, popular opinion in the Argyll was clearly with him.

'If you hold this place in such evident contempt, why do you burden us with your presence?' he said loudly.

Terence faced his accuser and delayed his reply for a second or two just to silently express disdain for question and questioner. He took a sip at his drink before speaking.

'Well, little man,' he said, 'I'm afraid I have no ready answer for you. The closest approximation to the truth is that my visits constitute some modern form of *noblesse oblige*. It's a version of that particular sentiment adapted to the present meritocratic times, whereby those successful in life return to their humble roots to inspire the less fortunate to greater efforts by their example. I should also say that my motives for returning are slightly selfish, again in accord with modern times, in that a certain piquancy is added to my sense of achievement by observing those left behind in the game of life. Alternatively, it could all be some obscurely motivated masochistic exercise in which...'

'Enough' said Mr Disvan, very quietly. Terence's deluge of wordy sarcasm straightaway ceased.

'Your presence we tolerate out of charity,' Disvan continued, 'but the ill feeling you generate is unacceptable. If you don't amend your manners, you'll have to go.'

Although temporarily subdued, Terence the solicitor was still full of aggressive spirit.

'Go, eh?' he said. 'And who'll make me?'

'I will, if necessary,' replied Mr Disvan, with a confidence their disparate sizes did not justify.

'And with Lenin snapping at your heels—if I can get him out of the cellar' added the landlord.

Terence's response was pugnacious in content, but nevertheless his tone showed that he had backed down from immediate confrontation.

'You people amaze me,' he said. 'You have no idea, no idea at all of a greater world outside this village, do you? Do you realise that with my influence and friends I could... I could have the Argyll's licence revoked, or even have a road driven through it. Hell's teeth, if I put my mind to it I could probably get the Ministry of Defence to put in a request to have this whole area as a training ground for the next hundred years! And yet you threaten me?'

'We've made no threats, Terence,' said Mr Disvan, 'and no doubt you could do all you say. However, have you considered what we could do with what we know about you?'

Once again Terence suddenly fell silent as the grave, restraining expression of his obvious exasperation to a mere angry glare.

'Ah, I can see that you have given it consideration,' said Mr Disvan. 'Very wise in your circumstances I must say. Doctor Bani-Sadr, would you care to examine our friend, please?'

'Gladly' said the Doctor. He advanced on Terence and sought his arm.

Terence spiritedly withheld it until Disvan fixed him with a look and somehow brought about compliance. Bani-Sadr held the tall man's wrist and took his pulse.

'Just as before,' the Doctor said, 'nothing at all, not a peep.'

Terence wrenched his arm free, quite beside himself with an anger that he did not dare, for some reason, to release.

'You're a quack,' he said to Bani-Sadr who received the insult with unruffled calm. 'You don't know the first thing about medicine. You ought to be struck off—in fact I'll...'

Mr Disvan directed a finger at him in warning.

'I'll... take my drink outside into the garden,' Terence ended weakly.

Dragging the bemused Cheryl with him, he strode off towards the door. His mind was presumably working furiously all the way there for, on the point of leaving, he came to an abrupt halt and turned to address us again. Cheryl, in tow, bumped into him and spilt half her drink.

'If I ever hear reports of loose talk about me emanating from you lot, you'll see that I wasn't joking about the M.O.D. training ground. Also my lawyers are pretty hot on unsubstantiated libels about me and...'

'Don't be silly,' replied Disvan, calmly. 'Go and have your drink and simmer down, there's a good chap.'

Terence clearly considered replying to this but decided not to. With a very graceful and eloquent gesture, he snapped his fingers at us and carried on out of the bar.

After such an atypical scene, the silence left behind was oppressive and conversation slow in restarting. Nobody however seemed very surprised by what had happened, and my curiosity was aroused by this.

'Who was that?' I asked Mr Disvan.

Terence Leander,' he replied, 'or Terence the solicitor as he was always known around here—that being the most important feature of his personality.'

'A local man?'

'Very much so. His family's name crops up in the old time church registers and militia lists with monotonous regularity. Terence, however, has severed himself from his roots to all intents and purposes. Once he qualified, he headed straight for the bright lights and the money of the metropolis.'

'Not to mention the shady deals of the metropolis,' said Mr Wessner.

'Ah, well, that's supposition,' said Mr Disvan.

'That's not what the fraud squad said,' Wessner persisted.

'He was acquitted.'

'On a technicality.'

Disvan shrugged his shoulders, conceding the point.

'Anyway,' he continued, 'Terence comes back from time to time, either on business or to flaunt his financial success.'

'Or to gloat,' said Doctor Bani-Sadr.

'Or as the doctor says. I must admit that his visits are hardly something I look forward to.'

'His old mother has barred him from her house,' added Lottie in support of the evidence so far.

'So they say.'

'What's the matter with him, then?' I asked.

'He's dead,' answered Disvan.

'I beg your pardon?'

'He's dead. You know—deceased.'

'But how... I mean—he's just...'

'Bought a drink and talked to us? Yes, I know, but that doesn't alter the fact that he's certainly dead.'

'That's right,' said Doctor Bani-Sadr. 'There's no pulse, no heart beat, no respiratory function, no electrical activity in the brain, no anything.'

'But how does he...'

'That's an interesting question that has exercised my mind for some time now,' said the doctor. 'I thought about doing a paper on the case for *The Lancet* but then it occurred to me that it wouldn't exactly help my career, saying that dead men walked the face of the earth when the dead man in question won't come in and own up to it. Accordingly I've just left it as a mystery.'

'My guess is that it's willpower,' said Mr Disvan.

'Yes,' replied Bani-Sadr, 'that could be so; the

prolongation of pseudo-life by sheer willpower. Mind you, that's perilously close to accepting the notion of a soul or non-physically-based awareness and other such nonsense.'

'Your atheistic faith is touching, doctor,' said Disvan, 'but...'

'Just a minute,' I said, interrupting the theological debate that would doubtless have ensued. 'I just can't believe we're having this conversation. Did you really say that man was dead?'

'Oh yes,' said Doctor Bani-Sadr, 'quite dead. I was there when he went.'

'You were?'

'Yes indeed. I was his doctor from the first time he complained of chest pains and his heart condition was diagnosed. I was called when he had his second heart attack and died.'

'What happened?'

'Much the same as usual in these cases, except that he was more talkative than most. I'd done all I could but he was obviously on the way out, and I didn't think he'd make it to the hospital. All the way there in the ambulance he was giving quite a speech, considering his condition, about how unfair it was that his career should be cut short. Mind you, he'd been like that all the time I'd been attending him, right from the first test, but on his death bed—or death stretcher to be more accurate—he was really... indignant. Yes, that's the right word. Indignant.'

'Terence was always like that,' said Mr Disvan. 'Even as a little boy he'd made up his mind what he was going to do with his life, and when—and woe betide anybody or anything in the way. Some people even said that he had a timetable of achievements written out.'

'It was true, he had. His mother told me,' said

Lottie, who was listening in on our conversation.

'I can well believe it,' said Disvan. 'Full of determination was our Terence. He never played games when he was a boy, which I thought strange at the time, and he never missed a day off school, passed all his exams, won prizes, and got his legal qualifications in record time. Life held great things in store for him.Which, I suppose, is why he wouldn't leave it when a dodgy heart disrupted his timetable.'

'That could be so,' said Doctor Bani-Sadr. 'He'd just become a solicitor when the heart valve defect was detected and things were starting to move for him. Also, that company of his was taking off after the Board of Trade decided not to press charges.'

'Wasn't that the napalm for South Africa incident?' asked Mr Disvan.

'Yes, I think so. He managed to seduce the civil servant who was investigating—or was that the investigation before? I forget now, but no matter. Anyway, all in all, in Terence's terms he had a lot to live for.'

I couldn't get enough of this. I was getting straight answers for once. 'And so?'

'So, a few minutes after I pronounced him dead in the ambulance and covered his face, the corpse sat up and said "NO!" in a very loud voice. Fair frightened the life out of his mother and the ambulance men, I can tell you—and me too now I come to think of it. Of course, I dashed over to see to him, and that's when I found there were no vital signs. He'd just decided not to accept death.'

'What did you do?'

'In such situations there's not much you can do. He was beyond needing my services, as you can imagine. By the time we'd got to the hospital and got the ambulance man down to a manageable level of hysteria— he was one of those university drop-out types—Terence was up and about, and he asked me if I'd see his mother home for him. I said okay, and then he just strode off into the night without another word. The next time I heard of him was about six months later in the context of a *News of the World* article about an executives' escort agency he was allegedly running. Of course, that was a long time ago, when he was making his first hundred thousand pounds and things sometimes were a bit... tacky, to say the least. That's all behind him now and he's the epitome of respectability—on the surface, and for a few layers below as well.'

The doctor sipped his barley wine ruminatively for a moment before returning to the subject to add a coda of his personal views.

'You should understand, Mr Oakley, that I mean no general criticism of someone not tolerating their death. No, not at all. It's just a pity that it's Terence the solicitor of all people who should be the one to manage it.'

'I can't agree with you there,' said Mr Disvan. 'All stories must have an end if they're to have a meaning.'

'Nonsense. For example, as far as we're concerned the universe doesn't end but even so, it does have a meaning.'

'Really, doctor?' said Disvan. 'How interesting. What is the meaning of the universe then?'

'It's—'

The doctor's statement, upon which we were all hanging, was cut short by the opening of the bar door and Terence the solicitor's re-entry. He seemed to have composed himself from his points defeat in the earlier verbal tussle and was smiling, if very insincerely, upon the assembled company.

'Two more martinis, if you'd be so kind,' he said.

The landlord looked at him suspiciously, seeking

some hidden barb in this request but finding none.

'Okay,' he said at length, and set about the drinks' preparation.

'So kind.'

Suddenly looking round, Terence caught my intent gaze upon him before I could avert it. Looking at me coldly, he called across the bar, 'I don't recognise you. What's your name?'

'Mr Oakley,' I replied, trying to appear undaunted and to forget just who or what was speaking to me.

'Newcomer?'

'Comparatively.'

'An old Binscombe family, though,' Mr Disvan interjected.

'Educated too,' said Terence.

'More or less,' I countered.

'I see. Well, Mr... Oakley, a word of warning to you. Don't believe every tale you're told around here. To these people the concepts of the seventeenth century would represent a mighty leap forward.'

A sense of loyalty whose existence was hitherto unknown to me was affronted by this remark.

'Is that so?' I said. 'In that case, I wonder if you'd permit me a favour, Mr Leander?'

'What is it?' Terence asked cautiously.

'I'd like to test your pulse and listen to your heartbeat.'

'Certainly not!'

'Why not?'

Terence sighed and said to no one in particular, 'On reflection I think the seventeenth century was a little too generous. Perhaps I should have said the eleventh century.'

'Perhaps you should go back to the grave where you belong,' said Mr Patel.

By now Terence the solicitor was halfway to the

164

door, drinks in hand. At this last remark he stopped and laughed loudly.

'Grave? Grave?' he scoffed. Why should I go to the grave? Next month I'm launching a new international company with projected turnover of five hundred thousand within a year. All in all, I'm worth fifty mil on paper. I employ over two thousand people in three different countries, and within a few years my parent company will go public. I have five houses, take fifteen weeks holiday and a new eighteen-year-old mistress every year—and you tell me to go the grave? You think of your lifestyle compared to mine and then tell me who's dead, eh?'

This might have been a telling point had the landlord not intervened.

'Don't sit out in the garden too long,' he said, 'it's getting chilly and you might catch your death.'

Amidst general merriment Terence the solicitor glared at him.

'You'll laugh on the other side of your face when the road widening plans are published!' he said and then stomped off.

'Well, there you have it,' said Mr Disvan when he had gone. 'Rich, successful, dead, and a bit of a charmer.'

'How come he's so successful?' I asked. 'Any solicitor can be prosperous but making millions is another matter.'

'Quite so,' Disvan replied. 'Well, in a funny way, you see, Terence's death was the making of him. Since he didn't need sleep any more after dying, he was able to devote twenty-four hours a day attention to his business interests. A profile I read in the *Financial Times* called him "the human dynamo", although whether he's a human any more is a moot point. Consequently, with that sort of industry and concentration, and Terence's particular blend of energy and unscrupulousness, all his ventures flourish.'

'Unless the law intervenes,' said Mr Wessner.

'Which it does less and less often as he gets richer and has less need for the more desperate sort of project. He's also acquired relationships of mutual interest with people "in high places" as they're called, and he and success now walk side by side.'

'Actually,' said Doctor Bani-Sadr, 'it may be he doesn't sleep because if he did, if his attention slipped for one second, his disbelief in his own death would be suspended.'

'And then he'd really die,' I said.

'Possibly. Or perhaps decomposition might set in,' the doctor agreed.

I went over to the window and looked out into the garden where Terence the solicitor, arm around his shrinking girlfriend, gazed lizard-like, unblinkingly at the other patrons around him. It was possibly an effect of my overworked imagination, but it did seem as if the sunlight around him was dimmer than elsewhere and that, in his immediate vicinity, laughter and good cheer ceased.

'Is his threat about the motorway and the MOD and so on, serious?' I asked.

'In what way?' said Mr Disvan.

'I mean, could he do it?'

'I dare say, if he pulled out all the stops and called in all his favours. He won't do it however, because, firstly we don't justify that sort of supreme effort, and secondly because he knows that a single word from us could ruin him.'

'Is he really that powerful?'

'Certainly. In a perverse sort of way we're almost proud of him, despite his unfortunate manner, seeing as he's Binscombe's most famous son. There's been talk in some of the papers that he might be a minister if he keeps on the way he's going. It was with that in mind that we tried to sell his secret to the Russian embassy—for the church roof restoration fund, you understand. Sadly, they wouldn't believe us.'

'Minister?' I said incredulously.

'Yes. Probably defence, given his links with the armaments industry, or maybe even Prime Minister. If he doesn't set the missiles flying while he's in office, he could end up in the Lords. Imagine that: Lord Binscombe!'

Quite suddenly the alien-ness created by the story I had just heard dissipated. That name and face was indeed familiar to me. I turned to look at Mr Disvan, and he could hardly have failed to detect the surprise and horror on my face.

'Do you mean that he's..?'

'Oh, didn't I mention that?' said Disvan. 'I assumed you'd know. Yes, Terence Leander is your local MP.'

Here Is My Resignation

Binscombe Station was too pleasant and restful a place from which to commence yet another day's hard labour. The commuters who waited there every morning, at least those who could still appreciate such things, were lulled into pleasant thoughts by the leafy surroundings and abundance of green all about. They temporarily forgot the painful wrench of rising too early and the spoilt pleasures of a hurried breakfast amidst the splendours of birdsong and the sunlight filtering through the foliage. Therefore, when their train arrived, it always came as an unwelcome intrusion of the mundane, workaday world into the beauty that was spread out by nature for all, if they would only accept it. The consequent hostile glares that greeted the train driver as he passed by the serried ranks on the platform had been a byword and cause for puzzlement among generations of railwaymen.

Constructed as a late Victorian afterthought in a time when there was no lack of cash and confidence, Binscombe Station had escaped later modification by management or German bombs and therefore remained much as its original designer intended. The building itself was of local Bargate stone, which gave it a warm, welcoming aspect and, in line with the thinking of the age of their construction, the doors, windows and guttering had been used to ornament and beautify as well as merely serve their basic purpose. Gracious features such as a ladies' waiting room and colourful flowerbeds were still maintained by the staff who, being largely local men, were rarely rude or offhand to travellers. All of which is to say that the station had clearly survived past its time.

It was set in a deep cutting through a chalk outcrop and could barely be seen from the main road which ran nearby. Similarly, trains came upon it almost by surprise as they rounded a tight curve, traversed a short tunnel and found themselves, without much warning, at a station on the outskirts of a village. To the stranger and the uninitiated, this phenomenon was the cause of many a rushed disembarkation and a small mountain of forgotten luggage over the years.

A great variety of trees and shrubs had found a foothold (or roothold) in the soil on the sides of the cutting and, by and large left alone by British Rail, they flourished to provide a green sward on either side of the station. In summer and autumn, passengers on this small part of the line could be forgiven for thinking that they were travelling through the centre of a wood instead of a busy part of an increasingly busy world.

Because of these qualities, Mr Peter Pelling had a great fondness for Binscombe Station and he did not begrudge the time he spent there each and every week-day. Some days he would even arrive earlier than necessary so as spend a few extra minutes in enjoying its atmosphere before being conveyed off to his daily combat in London. Mr Pelling's glare at the train driver each morning, although he was quite unaware of making it, was one of the fiercest the man had to receive.

Pelling had lived in Binscombe for nearly ten years at the time of this tale, subsequent to his tiring of the burglaries and noise in his previous home in London.

He had never regretted the change, although the commuting was somewhat irksome. What he did notice after the move, however, was a slowly growing reluctance to spend his days as he did. He had first ignored the emotion and, when this policy failed to still its voice, had analysed it *ad nauseam* without satisfactory result.

Within it there was a dislike of the metropolis and its people, certainly. There was also an element of boredom with his work and colleagues, but even together they did not nearly add up to the spirit of anger he felt. Mr Pelling resented the time he had to spend working to pay his mortgage and, although he had no other great projects or interests in mind, he felt a burgeoning sense of loss or waste with each hour spent in gainful employment. In this frame of mind he saw, or thought he saw, through the facade of purpose to glimpse the utter futility of the company in whose service he had spent his life. Feeling something of a hypocrite (for he still drew his salary) he went on a one man go-slow but found it went unnoticed. In rash moments he even threw one or two minor and untraceable spanners into the company's smooth operations, but no one cared overmuch. At the age of forty-five, with an impeccable name and not unsuccessful career record behind him, Mr Pelling had become as rebellious as any mohicanned punk or class war activist. Since he did not feel at home with either group he searched around in books until he came up with the title 'Nihilist' to describe himself. This seemed to fit rather well, although it brought him no pleasure.

On this particular morning, Mr Pelling felt especially discontented, and the fact that he was resigned to his fate only intensified his fractiousness. At 10:00 a.m. he was due for a meeting with an important client famed for his aggressive and patronising behaviour. Mr Pelling would have to grit his teeth and feign interest in the man's torrent of drivel as he had done many times in the past, while the client satisfied whatever curious itch made him behave in this way. Though he despised himself for it, Mr Pelling knew he would act as a company man should. There was too much at stake for him not to.

Pelling always stood at the same spot on the platform. A short period of experimentation had led him to believe that from there could be had the most pleasant view while he waited, and the greatest chance of a seat on the train when it arrived. None of the more chatty commuters or notorious nose-pickers or coughers waited near the spot in question, and therefore Mr Pelling felt that boarding the train from that point made the best of a bad job.

A dense and wild thicket grew right down to the platform's edge, and quite often Mr Pelling chose to turn about and study the abundant life therein rather than look at the opposite side of the cutting. There was generally something interesting to see there, be it animal, plant or an unusual piece of litter deposited by man or wind. Mr Pelling liked to watch the bees or butterflies that visited the thicket or the wild flowers and tall weeds that made it their home. Because he didn't ponder the matter too deeply, he envied the birds, insects and flowers (and even the occasional cat) their liberty and freedom from stress, and he wished that somehow society could be changed, preferably right now, so that man could live that way too. Just then the train would generally arrive, and Mr Pelling would dutifully board it and take his cosmic discontent to London.

Today, as has been said, Mr Pelling was particularly dispirited, and so turned naturally to the thicket for an all too brief look at what real life was up to. He was shocked, to say the least, to see that a far from natural pair of eyes were regarding him from the very depths of the greenery.

Pelling looked quickly around to check that he had not been spirited away to some other place, but found that he was still in the reasonably reassuring normality of Binscombe Station. Other commuters were beginning to arrive, cars were pulling up in the car park, and all was as it nominally should be. He turned again and found that the eyes were still fixed unblinkingly upon him. He had half hoped that they would have disappeared so that he could dismiss the incident as mere fancy, but that was hardly possible now.

They were of a slightly luminous yellow colour, almond shaped, and had no pupils that he could detect. It was difficult to discern their owner's form through the dense vegetation but Mr Pelling thought—though how could it be?—that he could just see a slim, humanoid figure crouching there.

'Er... hello,' he said uncertainly.

There was no immediate reply but, perhaps half a minute later, a slim white hand snaked elegantly out of the bushes and, with the motion of one gold be-ringed finger, beckoned Mr Pelling forward.

Pelling now noticed that there were perhaps a dozen or so pairs of eyes, identical to the first he'd seen, in a semicircle in front of him.

'What do you want?' he asked with commendable, if counterfeit, calmness.

The voice that replied sounded very, very old and yet still at the height of its powers. In tone it was like the most beautiful—but heartless—music; like a requiem composed by a high demon.

'Mr Pelling,' it said, 'we've watched you for a long

time. Now we'd like to put a proposition to you.'

* * *

'What's up with that bloke?' said Mr Oakley. 'He's talking to the hedge.'

Mr Disvan looked along the platform at Mr Pelling but did not reply.

The two men were travelling to London together by arrangement, for reasons of company. Mr Disvan intended to visit his stockbroker and then make use of the facilities of the British Museum library, to which he had some power of access. Mr Oakley was journeying on a peace mission, one judged sufficiently important to take time off work, to his mistress-cum-fiancée of the moment. To make a full day of it, they had agreed to travel early on one of the commuter trains.

'Look,' Mr Oakley continued. 'He's thrown his tie away—and his briefcase!'

'Well, well, well,' said Mr Disvan, 'I haven't seen that for donkey's years. So they're still around, are they?'

Mr Oakley was about to ask just who 'they' were but was prevented by the spectacle of Mr Pelling's sudden dash into the thicket, heedless of thorn and briar, and his eventual disappearance from sight. For a little while the crash and clump of his progress up the side of the cutting could be heard but then this too faded. Mr Oakley thought he could just detect, at the very limit of hearing, a shrill and triumphant keening (if that is not a contradiction in terms) but this also soon passed away—if it had ever existed.

'What on earth's going on?' he asked

'Nothing to worry about' said Mr Disvan cheerfully. 'Just another one away with the faeries.'

A Video Nasty

'Would you like to see a video, Mr Disvan?' asked Esther Constantine.

'That rather depends,' he replied. 'What's it about and where's it being shown?'

'It's a mystery sort of video,' said Esther's sister Dorothy, 'and it's being shown at our house not two hundred yards from here.'

'I didn't know you had a video machine,' said Mr Disvan with a note of surprise in his voice. 'I wouldn't have thought it was your sort of thing.'

'Oh yes,' said Esther Constantine, 'we couldn't be without it nowadays, could we, Dorothy? The television companies seem to put on all the best films at an hour way past our bedtime, so we record them and watch when it suits us.'

'And it's a film you want me to see is it?' asked Disvan.

'Not exactly,' Esther answered hesitantly, as if choosing her words with great care, 'but we're sure you'll find it interesting nevertheless...'

'Well, you've intrigued me sufficiently, ladies, in which case I'll accept your offer. Do you want me to come now?'

'Yes please,' the sisters said in unison.

'Very well, I'll just finish this drink and then we'll go. Can Mr Oakley come too?'

'Oh yes, he'd be more than welcome,' said Esther Constantine.

'Good. How about it, Mr Oakley? Or are you meeting one of your lady friends tonight?'

'No, I'm not,' I replied, 'I'm in between "lady friends" at the moment.'

'Is that right?' said Disvan, surprised for the second time that evening, 'It's the first occasion I've known that to be so.'

'Well, I'm working on the problem. A small rest is probably no bad thing.'

Mr Disvan considered my throwaway comment for a brief moment and then nodded his agreement.

'You could be right. You're not getting any younger, and reckless promiscuity is quite draining, I should imagine.'

If spoken by anybody else, I would have taken exception to this, but it did not seem worth crossing swords with Disvan on his unfortunate choice of vocabulary. The Constantine sisters, stereotypical elderly maiden ladies to a T, whom I might have expected to be shocked by Disvan's description of my alleged lifestyle, had either not heard what was said or ignored it. Accordingly, in the interests of peace, I let the incident pass.

'Thank you, ladies,' I replied, 'I will come and see your video. What is it about—a horror film?'

'That's how we'd describe it, but your judgement on the matter would be much appreciated.'

'All of a sudden I don't like the sound of this,' I said to Mr Disvan, *sotto voce*.

'Oh, come on, Mr Oakley,' he replied at normal volume, despite my attempt at discretion, 'where's the danger in being a film critic and, more to the point, where's your sense of adventure?'

'In common with my love life, it's enjoying the benefits of a short rest.'

Mr Disvan smiled but otherwise ignored my half-hearted protest.

'Well, if that's the situation, say no more, ladies, but lead on,' he said with mock gallantry.

This they duly did and we trailed behind them, leaving the warmth and comfort of the Argyll, out into a wintry Binscombe where a mist had arisen and each street light illuminated only its immediate area, leaving pools of darkness in between. As the sisters had said, their house was mere few minutes away, but I was already chilled to the bone by the time we arrived and therefore very glad to enter in. My relief was short lived for, as in many of the older Binscombe households, only one room, the 'living' room as it was aptly called, was heated. The temperature difference elsewhere between inside and outside was minimal—or so it always seemed to me, child of a centrally heated upbringing.

Even so, in deference to good manners and defiance of good sense, I removed my coat as soon as I passed through the door and waited politely in the chill hallway for permission to move on to the relative comfort of the inner sanctum. I noticed that Mr Disvan, presumably the product of just such a home, did not share my urgent desire to adjourn to warmer climes.

At last we were ushered into the living room and various refreshments were procured for us. The Constantines then sat down and exchanged glances as if each was prompting the other to speak. A long silence ensued, since neither was apparently willing to take the lead, and Mr Disvan eventually had to kick-start the conversation.

'Right then, ladies, what about this video you want our opinion on?'

Esther Constantine drained her glass of sherry and took the role of spokesperson while her sister looked on, ready to add anything she thought relevant.

'The video,' she said, 'is in the machine ready to play. But first a word of explanation so that you'll understand what we're on about.'

'Otherwise it won't be clear at all,' interposed Dorothy.

'Quite,' Esther continued. 'Well, the gist of the matter is that several nights ago we wanted to see a film that was on till rather lat,e and that being so we decided to record it and watch it the next day. Nothing unusual about that you may say, and quite rightly. However, since we're not too clever with machinery, we've never bothered with learning to use the timer and we just let the recording go till it runs out of tape, do you see?'

Disvan and I nodded solemnly while I wondered why we were being told all this domestic piffle.

'Well, in that way we came not only to record the film we wanted but also the final weather forecast, the epilogue and nearly an hour of nothing after the station had closed down for the night.'

'Or so we thought at the time,' said Dorothy.

Esther Constantine looked at us for some reaction to her sister's mysterious comment, but we maintained poker faces and she was thus obliged to press on.

'Exactly. As it turned out, though, when we came to watch the film the following evening, we found that we'd recorded something else as well.'

'Something horrible,' Dorothy explained.

'I presume you don't mean the epilogue,' said Mr Disvan.

'No, we don't,' said Esther, 'although that slice of religious mumbo-jumbo could well be described as horrible. It's something else we're talking about.'

'What precisely did you record, then?' I asked.

'That's what we're hoping one of you might be able

to shed some light on. What happened, you see, was that my sister and I watched the film and then started to get ready for bed—locking the house up, laying the breakfast table and that sort of thing. The television had been left on whilst we were doing all this and when we came back into the living room together we saw that... Well, something else had come onto the screen.'

'And there shouldn't have been anything there, because I'd heard the announcer say goodnight and the national anthem playing long beforehand,' said Dorothy.

'And what was it?' asked Disvan.

'See for yourself,' Esther Constantine answered and, taking up the bulky TV remote control device, she simultaneously turned the television on and set the tape playing.

We caught a few brief seconds of a clergyman reading a poem by D. H. Lawrence, this presumably being the end of the much discussed epilogue, before the calming tones of a young man wished us a goodnight and urged us not to forget to switch off our sets. The swirling sounds of 'God Save the Queen' (impermissibly accompanied by bagpipes) followed for a mercifully brief period. The transmitter then shut down and the screen was given up to random static.

'Now you have to wait a while,' said Esther.

This we did, as patiently as possible, while boredom quickly set in. I pondered if I should ask for a replenishment of my glass by way of reward for this unexciting task, but it seemed inappropriate to break the silence and sense of anticipation in the room. Looking to Mr Disvan for some guidance on whether to take this whole situation at all seriously (for his acquaintance with the Constantines was of long standing), I saw that he was paying keen attention to the twitching lines on the screen. Accordingly I went along with the game and pretended to study the interference for 'horrible' apparitions.

At some point, after the elapse of what seemed like a very long time indeed but was probably only a quarter of an hour or so, I must have looked away for a second. A sharp intake of breath from the Constantine sisters caused my gaze to snap back to the television and I saw that something had come on to the screen.

It was a person's head and shoulders, that much was certain, although the face was very indistinct, 'as if only half finished' as Mr Disvan later put it. In my more prosaic way, it looked to me very much like a man with a stocking mask over his head, filmed through a cloud of oily smoke on a camera that periodically slipped in and out of focus.

Whatever it was seemed angry, and mouthed violent words that were only occasionally audible, and then only as an incomprehensible muffled noise. For a few seconds the face or whatever it was suddenly came very close to the screen, shouting with extra vigour, and we all involuntarily shifted back in our seats. Then, just as abruptly, the vision retreated at great speed, as though propelled backwards, and receded into a dot and then invisibility. The normal empty picture, occupied by static, returned.

Esther Constantine turned the tape off with the remote control. 'That's it,' she said.

'Well, what do you think?' asked Dorothy.

Mr Disvan considered for a while, sipping the glass of vodka he had been given.

'Yes,' he said at length. 'It is rather horrible, wouldn't you agree, Mr Oakley?'

'Yes, I'd broadly go along with that,' I replied.

'Of course, we're both obliged for your critical opinion,' said Esther, with just the hint of irritation in her voice, 'but we were somewhat hopeful that you might suggest some form of explanation as well.'

'Oh, I see...' said Mr Disvan, genuinely surprised, as far as I could tell, at this extra demand on him. 'Well, I presume that you both discount any supernatural interpretation to what we've just seen...'

'Naturally,' said Esther, in a firm voice.

'No, that's not tru,e' Dorothy interrupted boldly, plainly having to steel up her courage to contradict her sister. 'For once there's no answer to be found up there.'

She point to the serried ranks of Marxist classics, from *Das Kapital* to Marcuse's *Eros & Civilisation*, which lined the bookcases along the wall behind us. I'd vaguely acknowledged their existence on entering the room but failed to notice the titles, assuming, in a most narrow minded way, them to be a random collection of *Golden Treasuries* and volumes about the Royal Family—the Christmas and birthday gifts of two long life-times.

I must have appeared a little puzzled, for Esther Constantine thought it necessary to explain their literary tastes.

'My sister and I have been Party members since way back,' she said, 'we've still got our Party cards, though sometimes I wonder what for exactly. We used to be typists at *The Daily Worker*, back in the days when it was a real paper, not some milk-and-water, Social Democratic rag.'

'That explains the ANC poster in your hall,' I said, 'I did wonder about that, I must admit.'

'And now that you understand,' prompted Mr Disvan, 'perhaps you could suggest a rationale for what we've just seen. An explanation that is sufficiently in keeping with the tenets of dialectical materialism to satisfy our hosts.'

I racked my brain for something plausible to offer, but only came up with feeble theories, easily shot down in flames.

'Intrusion from another channel?'

'Not at that time in the early hours,' said Esther, decisively.

'An illegal, pirate channel?'

'They wouldn't get much of an audience with that standard of show, and anyway, I rang up the IBA monitoring service. There was no such unofficial broadcasts that night.'

'A fault on the tape? A snippet of a previous recording?'

'We've used it before without anything showing up.'

'Um... how about a freak effect whereby cockpit transmissions from planes passing overhead are picked up by your aerial?'

Esther was scornful now.

'Oh, come on , Mr Oakley; we might as well say it's a ghost and be done with it as accept that.'

'Sorry, I was clutching at straws there.'

'I should think you were.'

Disvan's face was occupied by a smug smile.

'It's a bit of a puzzle, isn't it?' he said.

'And so it will remain if you don't assist,' said Esther Constantine sharply. 'We expected more of you. Don't forget you were a fellow traveller once, far more prominent that we ever were, so don't act all so superior.'

His smirk vanished instantly.

'You're quite right, ladies,' he replied, almost apologetic. 'I've no right to mock when you've asked our advice and we've freely agreed to give it. What would you like me to do?'

'Explain it away in some logical manner, for preference,' said Esther, 'but, failing that, suggest what we can do next.'

Mr Disvan licked his lips, more uncomfortable than I'd seen him for some while.

'Well,' he started, 'an explanation's not possible on present evidence, but presumably it would help if you could tell what the face on the screen is saying.'

'It certainly would,' agreed Esther, 'but the voice isn't clear, not even with the sound right up. We've tried that.'

'I don't doubt you have, but I've also got some facility with lip-reading. I didn't study him that closely first time round, but the face's mouth is fairly clear to see. So, if you'll kindly play the tape over again, I'll try and distinguish some words.'

'Where did you pick up that skill?' I asked.

'Oh, a long time ago' Disvan 'replied', as always avoiding any direct question about his past.

There was no opportunity to pursue my query, as Esther Constantine had started the video machine once more and Mr Disvan was studying the 'half-finished face' with great concentration. I also observed it, and found the experience no more pleasing second time around. In itself, what we were seeing was of no great moment—merely an indistinct head and shoulders mouthing words we could neither hear or understand. However, the overall effect was chilling because the figure clearly bore no good will to those to whom it spoke. It seemed to resent the moments when its image on the screen receded or drifted out of focus, and increased its vehemence of speech upon returning into relatively clear view.

A cold and unpleasant thought came into my mind to the effect (despite an entire lack of supporting evidence) that the face was watching us just as we were watching it. I was therefore exceedingly pleased when the second screening came, soon after, to its sudden end.

'Right then, Mr Disvan,' said Esther, 'what was it saying?'

Disvan ignored this direct question and looked at the sisters in what I can only describe as a suspicious manner. 'And you say that you know nothing about this thing at all?' he asked.

'No, not a thing,' Dorothy answered for them both.

'That's why we called you in,' Esther added.

'Well, I'm afraid I can't help you.' Disvan's tone was very final.

'But couldn't you tell what it was saying?' asked Esther, now very alarmed indeed.

'No, I couldn't. Not in any way that makes sense, at least.'

'So what shall we do, then?' Esther persisted.

'I suggest you simply ignore it. Wipe the tape and forget this ever happened.'

'That's hardly a solution,' commented Dorothy tartly.

Disvan was curt, almost angry.

'In the absence of a ideologically acceptable answer from the volumes behind us, it's the very best advice I can offer—and all you're going to get. Take it or leave it. Come along, Mr Oakley, we must be going.'

With that we departed from the house, leaving a fractious and uneasy atmosphere behind us. Out once again in the mist and cold, I challenged Disvan with what had just occurred, for I was—almost—as curious about the apparition as the Constantines.

'So what was the problem back there?' I asked. 'I don't think you're telling all you know.'

'A very common fault of mine, according to you,' he replied.

'It is, and you're doing it again.'

'Well, if you insist on an explanation, I'll merely say that I suspect that the Constantine's sins have found them out, to paraphrase the Good Book. If they were to be honest with themselves, they'd admit it and would thereby have the answer they want. And that, Mr Oakley, is my final and definitive comment on the matter.'

'Which in practical terms isn't the least bit enlightening.'

'Maybe so, but there again clarity isn't always a good thing. Far better to have your peace of mind.'

This statement also begged a number of questions, but I decided to let it pass. Bitter experience had taught me that attempts to wheedle information out of Disvan, once he had made up his mind to remain obscure, were a waste of time and effort. Resolving to take more care over the timing of recordings on my own video machine, I put the Constantines' problem out of my mind and rejoined the throng in the Argyll.

Later in the evening, I noticed Mr Disvan deep in conversation with Doctor Bani-Sadr, no unusual thing in itself but curious because of the privacy they sought and the deep seriousness of their manner. Both had grim expressions on their faces and the latter from time to time shook his head, vehemently denying something that Disvan was asserting.

Since the night was well advanced by that time, my thoughts lacked the necessary agility to connect this Binscombe summit meeting with the earlier part of the evening and I therefore paid it little heed. However, if I had known then of the horrible events which were to fill the weeks to come, I would not have thought their concern misplaced.

* * *

Prior to the video tape incident it was a rare thing for the Constantine sisters to visit the Duke of Argyll. They had, apparently, an old fashioned attitude towards being seen in a public house, and a strong disapproval of the landlord calling his dog Lenin. Following that particular evening, however, it seemed like hardly a day would pass without one or both favouring us with their company. On each occasion they would sidle up to Mr Disvan and attempt to engage him in a private conversation. He would listen to them for a brief moment and then, in an uncharacteristic gesture, dismiss both them and their tale or petition (for we were not privy to what was being said) with an impatient wave of his hand. Taking our lead from him, the other leading figures of the village similarly pretended that nothing was amiss and, aside from a friendly 'good evening', offered no assistance to the clearly troubled Constantines.

This went on for the best part of a fortnight, until one evening when the sisters entered the bar in such a state of distress that neither Disvan nor the rest of us could harden our hearts against them any longer.

Previously, the sisters had always maintained a facade, at least, of stern self control and forbearance, in keeping with their public image as educated and respectable pillars of local society. Now, though, it was transparently clear to all that some experience had rendered them careless of the impression they made.

Both came up to Mr Disvan and myself where we were standing at the bar. Esther Constantine grasped Disvan by the lapel and, controlling her feelings with difficulty, she said in a level voice, 'We'll beg, if that is what you require, we'll drag you there if necessary, but come you must. Things cannot go on as they are. We're in grave danger. We're comrades of old and it's your duty to help us.'

The fear and unhappiness on the old ladies' faces would have melted even a solicitor's hardness of heart, but Mr Disvan said nothing. He looked pointedly at the hand on his lapel and then at the supplicant Constantines—people whom I'd thought to be his friends. Something in his gaze caused Esther to release her grip.

'Please... for old times' sake?' hazarded Dorothy.

Disvan seemed set to remain implacable against the sisters until he happened to glance up and saw that all eyes in the Argyll were upon him and that he was surrounded by reproachful faces.

'All right, then,' he said. 'For old times' sake. Let's go and get it sorted out.'

* * *

'It's off now,' said Esther Constantine, pointing to her television set, 'but there's no telling what it'll do next.'

Mr Disvan and I (myself by special invitation) were once again in the ladies' living room and they were recounting the events that had brought them to their present state of fear. Mr Disvan was trying to piece together their scattered and disjointed testimony.

'You're saying, then, that the television switched itself on and the "half finished face" was on the screen.'

'That's right,' said Dorothy. 'On every channel.'

'How do you know that?' I asked.

'Because I used the remote control channel selector to try and get rid of it, Mr Oakley. How else?'

There was a sort of Binscombe logic to this that furrowed my brow even as I accepted it. Mr Disvan pressed on.

'What did the face say?'

'Gibberish for the most part,' Esther answered.

'Random words, inaudible phrases, hysterical laughter—that sort of thing.'

'And some profanity too,' added Dorothy.

'That also, and all in a voice that was neither a man's nor a boy's but some sort of mixture of the two. It wasn't even particularly human for that matter because it went up too high and down too low for a person's voice.'

'And how often has this happened?' I asked.

'To begin with, once an evening, but in the last week it's been getting far more frequent. Yesterday the face was appearing every hour or so whether the set was on or not.'

'Why not just take the plug out?' I asked, making what I thought to be a reasonable suggestion. 'There'll be no question of the set coming on then.'

The sisters looked at me with barely concealed contempt.

'That's hardly what we'd call a resolution, Mr Oakley; merely abject surrender,' said Esther.

'We're very fond of our television,' added Dorothy in an aggrieved tone. 'Why should we be made to give it up by that thing?'

I reflected that the Constantines' fighting spirit had soon been restored to them by their faith in Mr Disvan's assistance, and I henceforth kept my counsel to myself.

'Well, I still think that this problem is of your own making,' said Mr Disvan mysteriously, 'although a "resolution" of it may be more elusive and perhaps beyond you or anyone else. However, I've undertaken to help you, against my better judgement may I say, and that's what I'll try to do. Switch the set on and we'll wait for the face's return.'

'What good will that do?' said Esther.

The tone of Mr Disvan's reply was one of patience

and long-suffering rather than anger.

'I don't know, but it can't be any less use than standing here doing nothing, can it?'

The Constantines considered this for a moment and then as one, like a disciplined conspiratorial cell, nodded their agreement.

'I'll go and fetch some drinks and crisps,' said Dorothy, 'but I don't suppose we'll have to wait too long.'

* * *

I was in no hurry to renew my acquaintance with 'the half finished face', but as the evening wore on and we were obliged to watch a series of numbing, banal quiz shows and sitcoms, I began to wish Dorothy Constantine's prediction would come true. Disvan evidently shared my feelings, and after a while fetched down a weighty tome from the Constantine's book collection and flicked through that rather than watch the entertainment on offer.

'Tell me if anything happens,' he said, 'and I'll be right with you.'

Merciful release in the form of the epilogue came after what seemed like a geological age of waiting. Dorothy and Esther stirred in their seats and Mr Disvan closed his book.

'There's no point in us waiting here all night for something to happen,' I said, draining my glass thankfully. 'We can always return tomorrow evening.'

'That might not be necessary,' replied Mr Disvan, redirecting our attention to the television. 'Our guest has at long last arrived.'

It had indeed. The ghastly figure had silently come into view and was close up to the screen, mouthing and shouting as before. Occasionally it ebbed a little further back but, for the most part, the head and shoulders stayed put and seemed close enough to surge forth out of the television and into the room. Within a few seconds we could hear as well as see it, although what we heard made little sense—words such as 'get' and 'hate' and 'free'—all in a shrieking voice mixed with uncontrolled laughter and incoherent babble.

As soon as the figure appeared, Mr Disvan waved us to silence and began to study the face with analytical concentration. Despite their earlier distress, the Constantines seemed reasonably blasé about what was happening and looked at the screen with only mild distaste. In the present situation, since I was not permitted to speak, I could only give myself up to examining the apparition, and having seen more than enough of the figure itself, I looked closely at its surroundings instead.

At times the creature, or whatever it was, seemed to be standing in an endless landscape of high prairie grass over which a sky of disturbing shapes and colours rushed at alarming speed. For a while this would disappear to be replaced by a blackness of such intensity as to suggest that I was seeing the deepest part of the earth or a place so distant that no starlight reached it. The 'prairie' would then reappear.

Although I later thought myself credulous for feeling so, at the time I clearly felt that I had no business to be seeing these places. It was a distinctly uncomfortable sensation.

After two or three minutes, Mr Disvan said, 'Right, that's enough. Turn it off.'

Esther Constantine went to go to the television and do as she was bidden but Disvan prevented her.

'No!' he shouted. 'Don't go too near it. Turn it off at the mains.'

Esther hesitated, changed her tack and, crossing to the other side of the room, removed the plug from the wall. The television screen immediately went blank. It may just have been my imagination but I would have sworn that the sound of the thing's voice continued for a second, maybe two, after the power was pulled.

Fortunately, perhaps, I did not have too long to ponder on this fact for, soon afterwards, we were caused to jump by the ring of the telephone coming from the hallway.

'Would you see to that, Mr Oakley?' said Esther Constantine. 'At this time of night it must be a wrong number—or those double-glazing people.'

Glad of an excuse to leave the room, I went out and picked up the receiver. 'Hello, it's 12:30 at night, what do you want?'

The voice that replied seemed very distant and distorted by the line. 'Where am I?'

'Pardon?'

'I want to get out.'

'Who is this?'

'I want to live.'

I was about to say something that would bring the conversation, such as it was, to a decisive close, when it dawned on me that, allowing for the effect of the line, I had been listening to this self-same voice only a few moments before. Acting instinctively I held the receiver away from me. The speaker seemed to be aware that I'd done so, and now shouted so that I could hear just as well as before.

'I'll get you! [incomprehensible] I'm nearly strong enough! I want to live!'

There was long pause. Clearly the voice had nothing new to say, and I was too shocked to be able to alert the others to what was happening. Then, with renewed vehemence he or it began to speak again.

'Hate you! Not fair, not bloody [incomprehensible]. I'll pay in full!' Suddenly the tone of the voice changed dramatically from raging fury to plaintiveness. 'Where am I?'

At that moment, Mr Disvan looked round the door into the hall, presumably to see what on earth was detaining me. Gathering from the eloquent look of horror occupying my face that something was very amiss, he beckoned to the Constantines to follow him and approached the telephone. I gratefully passed the receiver to him.

'Hello,' said Disvan calmly.

Again there was a long silence before the voice bellowed forth once more in a tirade of foul abuse. Mr Disvan ignored this and again gently said, 'Hello...'

A gap of four or five seconds ensued. Then the voice continued in a still angry but more reasonable manner.

'I know all about you!' it said. 'I've been watching you. We all have.'

A long pause.

'I want to live. You are all [incomprehensible] long enough! I'm nearly strong enough! Before? Why? I'll pay you back! When I get... HA HA HA HA HA HA HA HA HA HA HA HA HA HA HA...'

The line abruptly went dead. The voice's final laugh echoed around the cold hallway.

'Has this ever happened before?' asked Mr Disvan.

The Constantines shook their heads, too shocked to reply in words.

We all returned to the living room and sat down. A contemplative silence reigned until Dorothy Constantine spoke.

'Come to think of it, though, Mr Disvan, we've had a lot of what we thought were wrong numbers lately—

that or burglars casing the joint—where there was just silence when we picked up the phone. Do you think..?'

'Probably, Dorothy,' Disvan replied gravely. 'Leastways, I shouldn't be at all surprised.'

Dorothy and Esther looked at each other in dismay.

'Anyway,' Disvan continued, 'I know for sure now what your problem is. The sense of what it was saying on the television was even clearer than last time.'

He paused and looked wistfully at the Constantine sisters.

'Well..?' said Esther in an animated voice.

'Are you sure there isn't something that you want to tell me first?' said Mr Disvan, ignoring the prompting.

'No,' said Dorothy.

Esther shook her head vehemently. 'No, nothing—get on with it, man!'

'As you wish. It seems that at some point in the past, there was a baby born in this house. It would further appear that the child was deliberately done away with very shortly after and buried somewhere in the structure of the building or perhaps the garden. What I was going to say was that it was laid to rest, but that wouldn't be correct. The spirit is very far from at rest. It has awoken and grown. It seems to want revenge and, worst of all, ladies, it seems to believe that you are responsible for its death and present plight.' He stopped to consider what he had said for a moment and then concluded, 'Yes, that's a reasonable summary.'

'Us responsible!' Esther Constantine exploded. 'Impossible!'

'Neither of us has ever had a baby, Mr Disvan,' said Dorothy Constantine, more mildly, 'and we would never dream of hurting one in any case.'

'Well, at least you're not denying the existence of a spirit. That's progress anyhow,' replied Disvan. 'But as for what you say, why should the creature lie?'

'Perhaps it's merely mistaken. Perhaps it's confused us with someone else,' said Dorothy.

'That could well be,' I interjected, already forgetful of the derision with which my previous contribution had been received. 'As a baby at the time of its decease, it would hardly be in a position to identify its killers, would it?'

'Maybe,' Disvan said dubiously. 'Maybe so. If things in its realm of existence are the same as here—which I doubt they are.'

'Mr Disvan,' said Esther fiercely, 'I don't give a tuppence for your opinion of our reputations but I tell you straight that neither my sister nor I has ever had a baby. In fact, the last babies born in this house were Dorothy and I, and as you can see we're both alive and well to report as much.'

'Well,' said Disvan, clearly still unconvinced, 'I hear what you say but, with your beliefs, I've always assumed that you were early proponents of free love and it follows from that...'

'Nonsense,' interrupted Esther, 'we've never subscribed to the glass of water theory.'

'The what?' I asked, somewhat bemused.

Mr Disvan enlightened me. 'A famous Russian revolutionary called Aleksandra Kollontai said that satisfying the sexual urge should be as simple and casual a thing as having a glass of water when you're thirsty. The phrase rather caught on.'

'Did the lifestyle that goes with it catch on too?' I asked, my interest engaged despite our present circumstances.

'Not really—although Kollantai practised what she

preached, even later on when she was the Soviet ambassador to Sweden.'

'Oh, I see.'

'This is all irrelevant,' said Dorothy. 'We've lived our lives according to the precepts of Lenin, not Kollontai—great feminist though she was—and Lenin said, "The absence of self-discipline in sexual life is a bourgeois phenomenon; wild excesses in sexual life are reactionary symptoms." And that is that as far as we're concerned. We've never practised free love.'

'Except,' said Esther, 'that Party summer school in Cambridge, just before the War.'

'Oh yes, I forgot,' agreed Dorothy. 'With the exception of that week we've never practised free love.'

'And there were no babies arising from it, either,' added Esther decisively.

Disvan pondered—and accepted.

'Ah well, if I was wrong for thinking what I did and for refusing to help you, then I ask your forgiveness.'

'You thought that we...' said Dorothy, shocked.

Mr Disvan shrugged his shoulders.

'What else was I to think? The thing was very adamant on the point. Admittedly, Doctor Bani-Sadr said that neither he or his predecessor had any knowledge of you bearing children, but in the time of your youth such things could be hushed up, couldn't they?'

Esther Constantine glared at him and ground her teeth in exasperation.

'Mr Disvan,' she said, 'you're an ill-thinking, suspicious old man.'

'Life has made me so,' he replied. 'However, to return to more pressing matters, if what you say is true then your only problem is to convince the creature. He seems to be hell-bent, if you'll pardon the phrase, on revenging himself.'

'And how do we go about that, may I ask?' said Esther.

'I've no idea at present, but I suggest that you start by leaving the television disconnected and not answering the telephone.'

'How about,' I hazarded, 'finding the baby's remains and giving them a proper burial, with a priest and everything, so that the spirit will rest?'

'Hmmm,' said Disvan, 'it's a thought I suppose, although I think that the significant difference in this case is that the spirit doesn't want to rest—quite the opposite in fact. We could have a look for any obvious place of concealment tomorrow. As for a priest, well, the Reverend Jagger won't help—not after that business with Trevor Jones's car. Do you know of a priest who'd help you, ladies?'

At that very moment the telephone rang. Esther Constantine looked at the hallway door in terror. Her gaze travelled in turn to Mr Disvan, to the silent television and to the bookcases along the wall. Then, with the profoundest of sighs, she buried her head in her hands.

* * *

'I've no sympathy with you,' said Mr Disvan. 'You should have followed my advice, at least for the time being, until we can think of something positive to do.'

'That's all very well for you to say,' replied Esther Constantine, 'but we particularly wanted to see that programme. We've watched the series right from the beginning and we couldn't bear to miss the final episode.'

'And did you get to see it?' said Disvan, in a manner that signified he knew full well the answer to his question.

'Thanks to that dreadful thing, no.'

'As I thought. So why bother, then?'

Dorothy Constantine shook her head. 'It's been a couple of days since anything happened. We thought that perhaps... Well, hope springs eternal. You know how it is.'

Mr Disvan's expression suggested that he did not. The arrival of the landlord disrupted the tense atmosphere of our little gathering.

'Would the ladies care to partake of liquid refreshment,' he said, 'or are they making use of my licensed premises, reckless of the crippling overheads it costs me to run it, as a free meeting house yet again?'

' "The ladies" will have two pink gins and none of your damn sarcasm, you mental pygmy,' said Esther Constantine in a machine gun onslaught of words that even bystanders such as myself, out of the line of fire, found intimidating.

The landlord flinched, faltered for a mere second and then bravely returned to the fray. 'If that's the way you feel, why don't you go and—'

'Enough!' said Mr Disvan, waving them to silence with a sweep of his hand. 'You can continue your old feud, if you so wish, in more normal times. Meanwhile, you two,' he indicated the sisters, 'can behave civilly to your host, and you,' (turning to the landlord), 'can show a bit of sympathy to people in trouble.'

This seemed to settle things, albeit not amicably, for the time being, and the landlord went off to fetch the requested drinks muttering, just loud enough so that he could be heard, that he'd 'call his dog what he bloody well wanted'.

'It was ghastly, Mr Disvan,' said Dorothy, continuing as if the interruption had never happened. 'This time the thing didn't say much...'

'Other than to growl and mumble under its breath,'

interposed Esther.

'...other than to growl at us, yes. But the worst bit about it was that the thing's face seemed to be following our actions—studying us, as it were—when we moved around the room.'

'Oh yes, it could see us all right, even if we can't see its eyes.'

'And as though that wasn't enough, the telephone started ringing.'

'And I suppose,' said Mr Disvan, 'that you answered it just like I asked you not to.'

'Not at first,' replied Esther staunchly, 'but it kept on and on, so in the end we did pick up the receiver.'

'We didn't think it could be any worse than what was on the television, you see,' said Esther in defence of their actions.

'Was it the creature on the end of the phone?' I asked.

'Yes, it most certainly was, and it said some really dreadful things.'

'Such as?'

'I'd rather not say,' said Dorothy primly.

'Suffice it to say, Mr Oakley,' said Esther, leaning confidingly towards me, 'that the voice expressed its hatred of us in no uncertain terms.'

'It's so unfair,' wailed Dorothy. 'We've never done anything to it.'

'Well, as you can imagine, by that time we'd had enough,' said Esther. 'I strode over to the wall to pull the plug on the damn thing.'

'Your first sensible move of the evening,' commented Disvan.

'Oh yes? Look what it did to me!'

Esther held up her right hand for our inspection and we saw that the tips of her fingers were covered in angry, red burns.

'Somehow, that vile thing had made the plug and cable live,' she continued, 'and it very nearly did for me.'

'Esther's hair had blue sparks in it and she had the shakes for hours after,' said Dorothy solicitously.

'Did you get it unplugged though?' I enquired.

'Not that time. Dorothy eventually went and got the rubber gloves from the kitchen for insulation and then used my walking stick to hook the plug out. You should have seen the shower of sparks from the wall and heard what the thing said whilst we did it!'

'So what should we do now, Mr Disvan?' asked Dorothy.

'Follow my previous instructions,' he said.

'No, apart from that, I mean.'

Disvan leaned back in his seat and pondered the matter for a moment in silence. The Constantines' drinks arrived and were downed in one.

My attention wandered lightly around the company gathered in the Argyll that evening and I sought, as before, to reconcile the strangeness of what I was hearing with the plain as-it should-be-ness all about. Just as before, I could not. These two streams of Binscombe life seemed to be separate and yet in close parallel. They were interconnected in ways that I could not fathom. There were bridges across the great void between them, but I was not privy to their whereabouts. However, many native Binscomites seemed to take these bridges' existence for granted and were able to cross them at will. No conflict or puzzlement was caused in the Binscombe world view (apparently bred in the blood) by the natural and supernatural lying down together like lion and lamb. I wondered whether I would one day aspire (or descend, depending on your point of view) to real Binscombe citizenship and share this frame of mind.

Mr Disvan then disturbed my idle reverie.

'Let's consider the possibilities,' he said. 'Our search of your house didn't turn up anywhere that might conceal a burial, and we can hardly dig up the entire garden. Consequently, the idea of putting the creature's remains to proper rest seems to be a non-starter.'

'Agreed,' said Esther.

Dorothy nodded her head.

'And I presume your objections to having a priest perform an exorcism remain as resolute as ever...'

'Absolutely.'

'Quite unthinkable.'

Once again I must have appeared bewildered by this, for the Constantines thought their stance required expanding upon.

'Yes, Mr Oakley,' said Esther, 'I know the situation we're in is hardly one covered by the thoughts of Marx and Engels but even so... I mean, if we're to go running, cap in hand, to some God-botherer at the first sign of something outside our philosophy, well, I ask you—what does that make of our lifelong convictions?'

I nodded my understanding.

'In that case,' said Mr Disvan, 'there's only one thing I can think of to do.'

'What's that?'

'Reason with it.'

* * *

On our way to the Constantine household, we all discussed Mr Disvan's proposed strategy, and he was able to overcome some of our early objections.

His simple argument was that there was no practical alternative to what he suggested—a point we found impossible to refute.

'If, as you say, you had nothing to do with his original death,' Disvan explained, 'and if, as seems likely, the creature is aware of what we do in this world, then perhaps the truth of the matter can be brought to his attention. Then, and this is introducing yet another "if", *if* the spirit or whatever is convinced that its attempts at revenge are misplaced, it may leave you alone.'

'I wish we could think of something better. Something a little less conditional,' said Dorothy.

'Something a bit more harmful to that disgusting entity occupying our house is what's really required,' agreed Esther. 'It goes against the grain to negotiate with an enemy such as that. We should be pressing for unconditional surrender!'

'That's the next stage if peace negotiations fail,' said Disvan. 'However, I strongly suspect that all out war would involve casualties before (and if) victory was achieved. Presumably you want to avoid that. After all, this isn't the revolution, and ghosts aren't part of the class enemy.'

He turned around and saw that his intended jest had fallen just about as flat as any piece of humour could. The Constantine sisters looked at him with expressions entirely free of amusement.

'Sorry,' he said and continued walking.

The evening was merely brisk rather than cold, and an absence of cloud cover allowed the moon and stars to illuminate the scene to a considerable extent. Looking ahead we saw that in the side street where the Constantines lived there were a number of vehicles parked: a police car and an ambulance both with their lights revolving, periodically bathing the nearby houses in an unnatural red glow.

'I should imagine it's old Mr Waddy, fallen down

his cellar steps again,' said Esther, sounding far from certain.

'I don't think so,' said Disvan, peering ahead. 'I can see movement outside your door.'

Mr Disvan was right, except on the point of detail that the Constantines' door no longer existed as such. Torn from its hinges, it lay useless and unregarded on the front lawn. Police and ambulance men milled about in the entrance to the house looking puzzled.

'What have you done to our house, you bastards!' shouted Esther Constantine as we hurried near.

Despite this, the long-haired leading ambulance man seemed pleased to see us. 'Here they are,' he said. 'Emergency over, lads.'

Needless to say, Mr Disvan seemed to know him well and, shielding the man from the outraged Constantines, he asked what was going on.

'We thought something had happened to the ladies,' he replied, addressing us in general. 'We had a report of a possible distress signal coming from the house. It was still going when we got here and, failing to get a reply, we had to take the door off to get in. Mighty stubborn door you had there, ladies, nigh two inches of teak—real old fashioned bit of workmanship. Shame it had to go.'

'What sort of a distress signal, Phil?' asked Disvan.

'Flashing lights. The house lights were being turned on and off in a regular pattern. As chance would have it, the old gent from across the way who reported it to us happened to be an ex-navy man and he said that the lights were spelling something out in Morse code, over and over again.'

'What?'

'Something like "help me" or "get me out", but you'd need to ask him yourself. It's a while since I was in the Cubs; I've forgotten my Morse. Certainly

201

the lights were flashing away in a very regular fashion when we got here, and they only stopped when we heaved the door off. I think you'd better get your wiring seen to, ladies, *tout suite!*'

'Crowbait!' Dorothy called him, by way of thanks.

'I see,' said Disvan, 'I see. Much obliged for your efforts anyway. Clearly it's a false alarm. Sorry for the call out.'

'That's okay, we'd have to be out and about soon anyway. Closing time's coming up.'

'Of course. Talking of that, how's Debbi?'

'Still drinking, I'm afraid.'

'Pity. Still, it's better than what went before, isn't it?'

'Never mind all that,' interrupted Esther Constantine, who had been boiling with silent fury all through the conversation. 'We don't want to hear your domestic trivia when we've got urgent business to settle. Come on, Disvan!'

'Suit yourself, lady,' said Phil the ambulance man, 'but it seems a bit late to attempt rewiring a whole house. Are you sure you know what you're doing?'

Both Dorothy and Esther withered him with a gorgon-like stare and then swept indoors, scattering police and ambulance men in their wake. Some half-heard abuse about 'running dog tools of state oppression' wafted back to us.

'I'll explain it all to you some other time,' said Mr Disvan to the assembled uniformed parties. 'If I'm able to, that is.'

Mumbling apologies to the public utilities and feeling somewhat sheepish, I followed him into the house.

* * *

'Did you manage to wedge the door into the gap, Mr Oakley?' said Dorothy Constantine.

'Reasonably well. It'll keep the draughts out till a carpenter arrives in the morning.'

'Thank you. Now Mr Disvan wants to see you in the kitchen.'

'What for?'

'I'm not sure.'

I walked along the hall, turned a corner and saw that Disvan and Esther Constantine were standing in the kitchen doorway.

'What's up?' I said, not liking the way in which they were clearly awaiting my arrival.

'Go in and see for yourself,' said Disvan, nodding towards the kitchen.

I was resolved to pass whatever sort of test this was with flying colours and marched in without another word, hoping that my inner doubts were not expressed upon my face. Standing in the centre of the room, I turned to see that Mr Disvan and the Constantines were watching me closely.

'Feel anything?' said Disvan.

'No, not really but—Hold on, yes, there is something, I feel like... like... I'm surrounded by static. A great field of static electricity.'

'I guessed as much,' said Mr Disvan. 'Your hair is starting to rise and there's sparks flashing off your clothes. Static would account for that.'

Once I allowed myself to perceive it, I realised just how powerful this feeling was. It seemed to be applying pressure evenly all over my body, producing a strong sense of tension and anticipation. My clothes felt as if they were floating free a few molecules above the level of my skin. By way of experiment, I went to touch the work surface near the sink and received a painful shock causing me to pull my hand away. The movement caused the atmosphere in the kitchen to crackle.

'Are you okay?' said Disvan.

'Yes, fine. It was just a mild shock, that's all.'

'So it's safe for us to come in, is it?'

'Yes, I suppose so.'

'Good, I was worried it might be something dangerous.'

I stared at Mr Disvan and the Constantines, who all suddenly seemed very alien and strange to me

'I thought that you'd already... Do you mean to say that you got me to walk in here to see if it was dangerous?'

Disvan and the two sisters looked at me as if unable to understand my outrage. He considered my question for a few seconds before replying.

'Yes, that's about the shape of it. Why, do you mind?'

I was temporarily lost for words and Esther Constantine stepped into the gap.

'It seems to be centralised in here but spreading all over the house. The whole atmosphere is charged.'

'And can you catch that low buzzing noise?' said Dorothy. 'I've heard it since we came in.'

We all listened carefully and realised that, just on the edge of audibility, there was indeed a persistent humming noise like that of a faraway machine, slowly warming up.

'Never mind that,' I said, crossing the room, crackling wildly and striking sparks in all directions. 'I want a word with you about using me as a guinea pig. What gives you—'

'Are you still going on about that?' said Disvan, an expression of mild surprise on his face. 'There are greater issues at stake here, you know.'

'Yes, don't be so selfish, Mr Oakley,' said Esther

Constantine. 'Let Mr Disvan speak.'

'As I was about to say,' Disvan continued, 'whatever it is afflicting this house seems to be using the power supply as a medium and has now become so strong and active that we can feel its presence all the time. Things are clearly coming to a head when its life force can seep out and pervade the whole building. Not only that, but it's starting to signal to the outside world—starting to draw other people into its story.'

Mr Disvan shook his head sadly. 'I'm afraid we can't have that happening. It mustn't be permitted. Everything's developing faster and worse than I expected—far worse, in fact. I never thought it would get this bad. It's now in my mind, you see, that the hate which motivates this creature is so strong that it could encompass and destroy more than just the Constantines. At the rate the child is growing, pretty soon it could spread further afield and find its way up other power cables—into other houses and in time into the main grid. Once it was running free in there, we'd never find it again.'

'Why the devil would we want to find it again?' said Dorothy Constantine, making what I thought to be a reasonable point.

Mr Disvan looked at her and spoke with a note of resignation in his voice.

'Think, woman. If it can do all this,' he waved his hand in the air to signify the house in general, 'drawing on just your power usage, imagine what would be possible if it had access to the National Grid. Imagine its strength if it found a power station, a nuclear power station perhaps, to take sustenance from.'

We started to imagine as we were bidden but Disvan interrupted our apocalyptic thoughts.

'Mind you, that's largely academic. If it got to that stage, none of us exist any longer. You ladies, Mr Oakley, myself, Binscombe—we would all have been swept away.'

He had succeeded in alarming me. 'Well, what shall we do? Do you still propose to reason with the thing?'

'I'll try, Mr Oakley, but I suspect it's too late for that. I think that all we can hope for is to placate it or kill it, but either way time is very short.'

'What do you mean?'

'Do you mean to say you haven't noticed?' said Disvan, pointing to the kitchen wall behind me.

I turned and saw that the hands of the electric wall clock were running backwards. They seemed to be increasing in speed with every second that passed.

'Time is reversing,' said Mr Disvan, 'back to the date of the child's death. And, unless I'm very mistaken, when that time is reached, it will be born again in this world.'

* * *

'Right then,' said Dorothy Constantine, grim faced, 'there's nothing else for it. Dorothy, go and plug the television in. It stays on till either we or the thing are gone.'

The screen came to life but nothing untoward could be seen. The ten o'clock news had just started.

'Should the Constantines be here?' I asked. 'I mean, if it's them that the creature wants...'

'It doesn't make any difference,' said Disvan absently, giving most of his attention to the television. 'You can't run from this sort of revenge.'

'Do you think this will be of any use?' said Esther Constantine, suddenly brandishing, to my utter, squeaking terror, an enormous automatic pistol.

Mr Disvan glanced at it for a second and then returned to studying the screen.

'No, I very much doubt it,' he said calmly.

'Mind where you're waving that,' I protested loudly as the weapon was pointed carelessly in my direction. 'Where the hell did you get it?'

'We're *Spetsnatz* reservists, Mr Oakley. Soviet special forces,' said Esther in a matter of fact manner.

'Well, even so, put it away. It's disturbing Mr Oakley,' said Disvan firmly, and Esther complied.

'Now go and check that the telephone's off the hook and that there are no other electrical devices on in the house. I want the creature's presence to be totally concentrated in the television.'

Dorothy went to do what was asked.

I looked at the set, yet paid no attention to the broadcaster's update on the coup in Chile.

'It's taking its time,' I said, hoping that my voice sounded reasonably nonchalant.

'Correction,' said Mr Disvan; 'it's biding its time. There's a world of difference.'

From upstairs there came a scream. I made to get up and go to investigate but Dorothy Constantine thundered down the stairs and rejoined us before I could stir.

'I've seen it,' she said. 'I went in the bathroom and when I looked in the mirror, the half finished face was staring out at me. It seemed like it was going to step out into the room.'

'I wondered where it'd gone to,' said Disvan. 'The last five minutes it was watching us from that mirror at the back of this room, and then it suddenly vanished. Obviously it wants to herd us all into the same place.'

The sisters and I hurriedly looked at the mirror in

question and checked it was blank.

'Why didn't you say that we were being watched?' I asked, a degree of irritation overcoming my fear.

'I thought that you were frightened enough as it was. We're all under observation every minute we're in this house anyway.'

'Well, I wish it would hurry up and come back,' said Esther.

'It has,' replied Disvan. 'Look closely at the screen. We've started.'

I looked and at first could see nothing amiss. Then, I noticed that one of the figures pictured on the set was not entirely as it should be. The picture showed a group of South African soldiers walking through the ruins of some guerrilla camp they'd destroyed. One of the troopers did not have a human head. Atop the pale uniform was the 'half finished face' and the figure was watching us, assault rifle at the ready.

The scene then changed to depict a meeting of the United Nations Security Council and again one of their number was the indistinct creature, although this time dressed in a smart, dark suit.

By now, the Constantines had grasped what was going on as well and they gasped in amazement.

'We wish to speak to you for one last time,' said Mr Disvan, 'before you are born.'

All the sound from the television abruptly ceased.

'And you die,' said the distinctive inhuman voice of the 'child', now seen as a famous footballer.

'That may be, but we still wish to talk.'

'Why?'

'We need to know want you want.'

'I want to live!'

'But you must know that is forbidden; you're dead.'

'I'm going to come back. I'm nearly strong enough now.'

'I said that you are dead, quite dead. Do you understand?'

'They killed me when I was helpless and put me in the wall.'

'Who did?'

'Mummy and daddy.'

The picture on the television changed. He was now a bishop at prayer.

'What were their names?'

'Mummy and daddy.'

'What were their names?'

Angrily: 'None of your business. They're dead and gone on anyway. They don't live in this place anymore.'

The Constantines, now justified, their innocence proven, gave me an 'I told you so' look.

'Then why do you hate these people here?'

'They're warm. I'm not.'

'But—'

'They didn't let me out.'

'How could they, when—'

'They're in my house.'

'But is it right to hate them?'

'There is no right or wrong. They do not exist.'

Mr Disvan shook his head, evidently despairing of his attempts to reason.

'Would it please you if we took you out of the wall and buried you properly?'

'Why bury me? I'm not dead. I'm not dead any more. I like it in the wall. Mummy and daddy put me there. I didn't see them again. Why bury me? You want to kill me.'

'No, we can't kill you. You're not alive.'

'I am alive alive alive, I'm a grown up boy now.' The creature was now seen as part of a UDR patrol in Belfast.

'How is that?'

'Your electricity warmed me, incubated me. I listened to all you had to say, I watched you through this screen and I learned. My mummy and daddy would be proud of me!'

'But must you come now? Why not wait longer? It's not a very nice world out here for a little orphan.'

'Isn't it?'

'Oh no.'

'But my friends will come too and look after me.'

'What friends?'

'There used to be a barrow here before my house and there's a chieftain buried in it—and a dog once died here too. They've both got warm and I'm persuading them to come out with me. They will help me kill you.'

'What will you do then?'

'I will live.'

'And..?'

'Pull this house down, pull this village down, pull everything down till I find where my mummy and daddy are hiding. I'll lurk in dark places and jump out and punish all the people who didn't help me out of the wall.' The voice giggled and laughed for a spell and then resumed. 'In a little while, I'll have all of me in this machine you're watching and then I'll come out and start by dealing with you.'

The television picture returned to showing only what it should: a weatherman announcing that tomorrow would be stormy.

'How right you are,' said Disvan.

'Quick, pull the plug out of the wall,' I said, 'before it can...'

Mr Disvan shook his head and, with a wan smile, pointed out that the whole area by the plug was clearly live. Small arcs of blue light were emanating from the socket and singeing the nearby furnishings.

'I'll warrant the fuse-box is just the same,' he said.

'You'd better go, Mr Oakley,' said Dorothy Constantine. 'This isn't your fight.'

'What do you mean?'

'Just that,' said Disvan, intervening. 'My efforts have failed. The creature is going to be born again and we've got to face the consequences. You needn't, however, so I suggest you go home and await developments.'

'I don't understand. What are you going to do?'

'There's very little time left, Mr Oakley, so I'll say it briefly. The child is going to come out and we'll be here to meet it halfway. It'll take us into its world and we'll continue the fight there—in the walls and cables of this house and wherever else it resides.'

'But... you'll be dead.'

'As we understand it, yes. But, in the kind of pseudo-life the creature exists in, we'll linger on—in its mind, so to speak.'

'And what are your chances there?'

'Slim, I should imagine.'

'Then why bother?'

'Because absorbing and fighting three people who are so aware of its nature will drain the creature. We'll set it back years in its growth, even if we can't destroy it from within.'

'Then I'll stay. Four is better than three.'

'Why? said Disvan coolly. 'You're not a Binscomite and even if you were one...'

Dorothy Constantine interrupted our argument by screaming once again.

'It's back!' she yelled. 'It's really close and...'

She was cut short and, as it turned out, silenced forever by a monstrous hairless forearm made of pink electricity which emerged from the television screen. It reached into the room and grabbed her by the throat. She wrestled with it for the briefest of moments and drew blood with her nails, all the while being dragged remorselessly towards the set. With a final tug the arm drew her in and they somehow passed through the screen and out of our sight.

Against my wishes, my eyes were drawn to the television. Horror mounted on horror as I saw that the view of the creature's prairie had returned and that the broken and twisted body of Dorothy Constantine lay amidst its long waving grass. Overhead the black and scarlet sky raced on like a movie backdrop.

'Me next,' said Esther Constantine. 'Cheerio.'

As if in answer to this 'request', the arm flashed forth again and lay hold of Esther's hair. She too began the journey to the screen and death.

Mr Disvan, up to now lost in silent observation, all at once came to life again and leapt to the side of the room with surprising agility. He scooped up an object and pointed it at the television. Although I was, by now, in no frame of mind to make rational judgements, I assumed he had gone to fetch the Constantines' gun in a rather forlorn attempt to kill something that had no life. However, instead of small arms fire, I heard only the slightest of clicks.

Turning to see if Esther had left us yet, I saw that the forearm was frozen still in the act of dragging her along and then that, miraculous to relate, a slight effort on her part succeeded in freeing herself. She reeled away to the back of the living-room and the arm hung motionless in mid-air like some vile gallows. A few seconds later, the forearm withdrew, at vast speed, into the set. Normal transmission interference filled the screen.

I started to realise that perhaps my life was not to end here after all, and with that came the recovery of speech—albeit not coherent speech.

'What did you... I mean, is it...'

Mr Disvan smiled broadly and by way of explanation held aloft the cause of our salvation. It was the television and video remote control device.

'It occurred to me, Mr Oakley,' he said, 'that when the spirit was wholly in the television and on the video channel, it was at its most vulnerable. Don't you see? I put the video on to play, froze the creature with the pause button and now I've rewound it onto a cassette. So long as I hold it on pause we're safe.'

'Is that logical?' I asked.

'It conforms to the logic of the phenomenon, Mr Oakley, that's all that's required.' For the time being I was happy, pre-orgasmically so, to accept his word.

'What about Dorothy?' asked Esther Constantine.

'Gone, I'm afraid. She's frozen on the tape with the creature.'

'Dead, in other words.'

'As near to it as makes no difference. I'm sorry.'

At the time—forgivably, I think in the circumstances—I was more concerned with staying amongst the living than remembering the dead. I interrupted Disvan's commiserations.

'Is it safe to disconnect the television now?' I asked.

'Yes, quite safe. Most of the creature's being is trapped in the video tape for the moment.'

'For the moment?'

'Well, yes. It'll force its way out in time, but we've got a while yet—perhaps a day or two before it burns the cassette up with its hatred and sets itself free. That gives us the opportunity to prevent a recurrence.'

After what had happened I had a lot of faith in Mr Disvan's estimate of our period of 'safety' but even so, did not waste any further time in turning the television off and removing the tape from the video machine. I do not think it was my imagination that caused me to detect undue warmth and an angry pulse in the cassette as I held it in my hand.

'Put it in the middle of the room, Mr Oakley,' said Disvan, 'as far away from the walls and any power cables as you can get it.'

'No,' said Esther. 'Give it to me that thing's got my sister on it. I'll look after it.'

'I don't think that's a good idea, Esther,' said Mr Disvan very firmly. 'Dorothy's not really anywhere anymore. Not the flesh and blood Dorothy we knew, anyway. Best put the idea of her survival, in any shape or form, out of your mind.'

Tears were now freely running down Esther Constantine's wrinkled face, although she allowed herself no other signs of distress. She seemed unable to take her eyes from the silent television set.

Mr Disvan now put on his comforting tone of voice.

'I should get to bed and get some rest, Esther,' he said. 'We've got a busy day ahead of us tomorrow. Don't worry, Mr Oakley and I will keep watch.'

She seemed not to have heard this and he was about to repeat it when the old lady suddenly came to. She looked hard at the remote control device which Disvan was still holding.

'It was a good idea of yours, Mr Disvan,' said Esther bitterly. 'Pity you didn't think of it just a mite sooner.'

He shrugged his shoulders as she went up the stairs.

'Three out of four survivors isn't bad. There's no pleasing some people, is there, Mr Oakley?'

* * *

'So you still won't allow an exorcism, then' said Mr Disvan.

'No,' replied Esther Constantine, 'I will not have a priest in the house.'

'And you won't move.'

'Again no. I was born there, I grew up there, and I intend to die there. Besides which, it wouldn't be fair on the new owners.'

'True, very true. We're very glad to hear you say that. We'd be sorry to lose you from Binscombe.'

'Thank you.'

'Still, if you reject all the alternatives, you've got no room to complain about the way things are. It was done for the best.'

'I suppose so, but it's damned inconvenient. To think I spent my life in hope of social progress only to come to this. It's like living in the eighteenth century.'

Esther indicated with her arm to take in both the room we were in and, presumably, her house in its entirety. I followed the gesture with my eyes, so far as the weak candlelight would permit, and realised that Esther Constantine had indeed effectively been pushed, much against her inclinations, several hundred years into our past.

'There were worse centuries to live in,' said Disvan.

'Really?' replied Esther dubiously.

Directly after the tragic death (or disappearance, as Esther termed it) of Dorothy Constantine, there had been a day of sustained destruction in the house. Electricians from the village, both hired and volunteers, had purged the building of every wire, fuse and cable and, as Esther had said, plunged it, in power terms at least, into a previous age. Subsequently, a kitchen range and various gas lamps were procured and installed, various kind souls repapered the ravaged walls: civilisation, of a limited sort, was restored. In due course the Electricity Board called, gave their bewildered approval to the work that had been done, and completed it by severing the house from the mains supply. The Constantine residence now stood in glorious isolation from the present era.

The video cassette, along with all the other, possibly tainted, electrical devices from the house, I buried in the garden. A ring of blackened grass that appeared a little while later above this spot was associated with the creature gaining freedom from its temporary captivity.

'Do you think it's still here?' I asked.

'Think?' Esther replied imperiously. 'Think? I know it is. Follow me.'

Mr Disvan and I did so and were taken to the kitchen. Esther opened a cupboard door, and to our surprise we saw that, atop a small black box fastened onto one wall, a tiny glass bulb was flashing furiously away.

'You see?' she said. 'It's here all right!'

'I hope that's a battery powered device,' said Mr Disvan.

'Yes, don't worry. I'm not stupid, you know. That filthy dead thing can only get 1.5 volts of itself in. That's enough for me to tell if it's there, but not enough for it to be able to do anything.

'It's almost good enough to read by,' I said, regretting it even as I said it. 'Not to mention a great way of recharging batteries.'

Esther looked at me more in pity than in anger and shook her head.

'Mr Disvan,' her voice was all bitter pleading, 'when will this nightmare end?'

He shrugged.

'It might not, although I suspect that one day it will. The problem is that time is different in the creature's world. It doesn't have any direct relation with our own. The thing has been "born", it has clearly grown and, by extension, it must someday "die", that I'll grant you. But as to when... it's anyone's guess.

'But,' she persevered, 'what if it outlives me?'

'We'll make sure you're put to rest a good way away where it can't get to you.'

'No, I mean what about the people who'll come after me?'

'There won't be any. You're going to make provision in your will that the house stays empty until such time as your executor says it can be sold—i.e. when that light stops flashing for good.'

'And who's that executor to be, may I ask?'

'Myself.'

'You seem to have it all worked out very nicely, Mr Disvan'

'And you of all people should appreciate the necessity of having it all worked out.'

Esther nodded, conceding the point.

'Mind you,' she continued, 'the light in the cupboard isn't really necessary. The creature's still alive in the walls. I only have to put a mirror up for more than a few moments and its ugly face appears in it.'

'I wondered where all the mirrors had gone,' said Disvan.

'Well, now you know. You see, the worst thing is... is...' she almost broke down, but by an effort of will recovered just in time, 'is that the thing doesn't only show himself. He shows images of my dear sister—horrible, detestable images of the two of them together.'

'I understand,' said Disvan. 'Listen, that bulb is sufficient for you to see if the creature's still about. Put temptation out of your way. Lose all your mirrors.'

Her strength at last exhausted, the old lady could

help herself no longer and she began to gently sob, her cardiganed arm across her face.

'I understand,' she said, between gasps of despair, 'I'll try and do that. But how will I see to brush my hair? How else will I see my sister?'

For once, Mr Disvan's voice was almost brutal.

'Where she is, I don't think you should,' he said.

Lightning Source UK Ltd.
Milton Keynes UK
UKOW032120211111

182437UK00003B/2/P